# On Macab␣

## Original railway tales to haunt the imagination

### Phil Mathison

Published by Dead Good Publications
Newport
East Yorkshire
HU15 2RF

©2013

1

# Other titles by the author

Shed Bashing with The Beatles
(ISBN 9780095469732)
The Spurn Gravel Trade (ISBN 9780095469763)
The Saint of Spurn Point (ISBN 9780956299406)
Tolkien in East Yorkshire 1917 - 1918
(ISBN 9780956299413)

ISBN 978-0-9562994-2-0

Published by Dead Good Publications
Newport
East Yorkshire
HU15 2RF

# Contents

# Introduction

In Britain, in the land of their birth, railways hold a special place in the heart of the nation. The supernatural, the ghostly and all things macabre have always excited and intrigued the mind. Together, these two topics, railways and the unexplained, exert a mysterious fascination. Over the years, I have written a number of short railway mystery stories and I present fifteen of them to you, the reader, hoping that you will derive as much pleasure from reading them as I have had writing them. Here you will find tales of murder, ghosts, demons and of hauntings played out against the backdrop of the steel rail, the whiff of steam and the clang of buffers.

A number of these stories have appeared in the railway press over the years, and I thank the relevant editors for giving them their first opportunity of an airing. That excellent publication 'The Railway Magazine' has published no less than seven of them. 'The Parliamentary' (a name given to a train that the company has to provide, and has to stop at all stations, which dates back to the very earliest days of the railways) in January 2000 ; 'Mental Block' January 2002 ; 'The Suspended Service' January 2003 ; 'Dead on time' January 2004 ; 'Terminal Illness' January 2007 ; 'The Curse of the Banker' January 2010, and finally 'Points of No Return' in January 2013. For pure nostalgia, the magazine 'Steam World' is hard to beat, and in the past they have reproduced three of my yarns in print : 'Fired Up' in December 2001 ; 'The Drewton Tunnel Possession' in December 2002, and most recently 'A Question of Timing' in December 2008.

Due to the pressure of space, the magazines have often edited the stories to fit the strictures of a monthly publication. Here you will find the tales in their original, uncut versions. For maximum effect, read them on a stormy winter's night, with the wind howling at the windows, and ideally in front of an open fire. A glass of wine may lubricate the juices of the imagination, but if you are of a nervous disposition, it could be unwise to indulge your curiosity while on your own!

Many thanks to Jim Bailey for help with designing the suitably ominous cover.

Phil Mathison

September 2013

# DEAD ON TIME

"Home for Christmas, or my name's not Jack Whiteley!"
That's what I thought to myself as I ran, hell for leather,
down the darkened lane to pick up the Carlisle -
Normanton goods at Kingmoor yard that Christmas Eve.
It was to be my final run over the Settle and Carlisle
line.

Well , for this year anyroad.

I was to drive the freight train to Leeds, where I was to
be relieved outside Holbeck engine shed by local men
for the last few miles.

I nearly hadn't made it, for I'd been tired all that day
and I'd overslept. Waking up with a jolt, I'd looked up
at the clock that evening, and realising that I was on
the late shift, I'd shot out of the railway digs and along
Etterby Road like a demon. However, the thought of
being home in Morley by midnight, and the clatter from
Kingmoor marshalling yard gave me fresh heart as I
crossed the running lines to where my train was waiting.
In the darkness, the warm glow from the loco cab seemed
like an invitation from an old friend. Half in shadow
and half in light, I could make out the face of the
fireman as he stoked up the firebox. On this trip, it was
Geoff Holmes who had been rostered for the turn. He
was a young chap that I'd never worked with on the
footplate before, though we knew each other by sight.

Geoff was working hard when I climbed up onto the
footplate, and his welcome was distinctly less warm than

the loco's cab.

"I'm Geoff Holmes" he said abruptly. "Just getting the fire ready for you. For a minute, I thought you weren't going to make it, Jack".

All the colour then seemed to drain out of his face, before he continued grumpily "You're a bit late. I really didn't want this shift either, with it being Christmas Eve."

I nodded an acknowledgement back.

I was never one for too many words, but I could see me taking it to an art form with this character. On a steam engine it wasn't always easy to be heard, and so a series of nods and winks was often what passed for communication.

Geoff looked across at me as he shovelled coal into the fire, and said "We're a bit down, so let's hope that we get a clear run. Want to be home in good time for Christmas!"

Aye, you're right, I thought to myself. In my mind I could see the decorations, the presents, the turkey, a chance for a lie-in. Yes, a lie-in, that'll suit me.

With that we got the all clear.

I wound the brake off, put the loco in full forward gear, and slammed the regulator open. The engine, an L.M.S. 'Black Five', seemed to lurch beneath our feet like a thing possessed, and sending a warning blast into the gloom, we were off. Off home.

The train gathered speed steadily through Carlisle Citadel station, and by Petteril Bridge Junction the exhaust was barking defiantly at the threatening December sky, as we rolled out into countryside. With sparks and smoke flying heavenward, the Eden Valley

7

opened out before us. There was a chill in the night air, and a hint of snow in the wind, but the loco was responding well as we ran down through Appleby at full speed.

I kept her 'wound up' for the long climb up to Ais Gill, running the locomotive as hard as I dared. The thought 'Home for Christmas' seemed to echo round my head in time with the urgent rhythm of the wheels.
The locomotive felt good under my feet. The tang of the hot regulator on my palm, and the warmth from the fire against my legs made the journey a pleasant one for me, but Geoff didn't seem to be seeing it that way.
"You know how t' mek work for your fireman!" he screamed indignantly at me, as he threw coal on relentlessly as we slogged our way up 'The Long Drag'. Our pace slowed as the gradient took its effect, but I kept her opened out, belching fire and smoke into the unrepentant blackness.
Yes, I was pushing the loco on, on home. Home for Christmas.

Now the summit is at Shotlock Hill Tunnel, and with the exhaust ricocheting angrily off the tunnel roof, the train pounded its way over the top, and onto the falling gradient. We gathered momentum as we ran on into Moorcock Tunnel, and with the quickening clatter of the rail joints tapping out our accelerating descent, we flew out of the tunnel portal at the other end.
I saw the look in Geoff's eyes as we passed the lights of Blea Moor signalbox and tore on. On into the menacing

8

fells and the night.

It was a look of panic.

"Steady on, mate!" he shouted at me across the footplate, as it rocked violently. "I know we want to be home tonight, but I'd prefer it if we got there in one piece!" He's a nervous type, I thought to myself.

The road had been clear all the way from Carlisle, but as we approached Settle Junction, the distant signal was at caution.

On the falling gradients, Geoff had had a chance to regain his chair, and leaning on his shovel, he looked across at me. In the cloistered space of the loco's cab, the glow from the burning coals lit up his brooding face like a Halloween mask, before he glanced apprehensively across at me and said "Jack, the distant is agen us, slow down."

Now, I had no intention of being home late if I could help it, and so I made the decision to keep her rolling, and just hope that the home signal would change in time for us to sail under it on green.

"Jack, for God's sake, we aren't going to get a clear run now. Slow down!" Geoff yelled menacingly.

I didn't, and as luck would have it, the signal arm rose up as if to salute us on our way, and we coasted under its welcoming green light at forty miles an hour.

"You could have got us both killed there!"

Geoff was not amused. By the terror in his eyes, you'd think he had seen a ghost. His face, not a pretty sight to begin with, was now as white as a sheet.

Definitely a nervous type, I thought. I won't be doing

any more turns with him.

With no further ado, we sailed under clear signals on through Skipton, and then I throttled the engine mercilessly for the final run into Leeds.

Soon, the protesting screeches from the wheels of the goods vans behind us told me that we were rounding the severe curve at Shipley, and before I knew it, we were rattling over the metals at Wortley Junction. On the pointwork, the unwilling cavalcade behind us rattled and protested one last time as I eased our train over Whitehall Junction, and came to a stand outside Holbeck locomotive depot. As soon as we came to a stand, the safety valves on the 'Black Five' erupted in an explosion of steam, as if to give me a final send off home. Home to Morley for midnight, I thought to myself. Home for Christmas.

I waved goodbye to my morose fireman, and I climbed down onto the ballast. From the look on his face, it seemed that Geoff Holmes was as glad to see the back of me, as I was to see the back of him.

"Glad to see the back of him!" muttered Geoff under his breath, which he'd only just had chance to regain. "I won't be doing any more turns with him!"

Handing over to the local traincrew, Geoff mumbled "It's all yours now".

With that, he climbed down onto the trackside as they took over the controls for the final stretch.

The fireman immediately started cleaning the fire and the driver checked the water level in the sight-glass, ready for the run on to Normanton. Behind him, as he stepped across the shimmering lines, Geoff could hear them chattering above the clatter in the engine's cab.

Striding purposefully towards him from the murk of the depot yard was the familiar figure of Joe Foster, the night foreman.

"You're dead on time!" came the cry from Joe, as he walked over to Geoff under the unnatural glow of the shed lights. A pall of smoke drifting from the steam locos fell over them as they met.

"We heard you were half an hour down leaving Carlisle."

"We were" Geoff blurted out "But that Jack Whiteley drives like the devil!"

"Jack Whiteley, you say" came an astonished reply from Joe.

"Yes, that's what I said, Jack Whiteley. I won't be doing any more turns with him, that's for sure!"

There was a pause, and Joe's face fell "You're dead right there, son".

As a fireman, Geoff had always been frightened that a bad word from a driver could hold him back from getting the driver's job he'd always wanted, and so he shuffled his feet, before hesitantly replying "And why's that?"

In the distance, a church clock struck midnight, and with light flakes of snow falling around them like angel dust, Joe's reply boomed through the still, frosty air.

"Because I've just heard from railway control that the landlady in Carlisle found Jack dead in his bed tonight!"

# FIRED UP

"Come on, Albert, give us a story!"
The regulars at the Bluebell Inn were in festive mood, and Albert liked to tell stories. In fact, when he was tanked up, he liked NOTHING better than spinning yarns to a good crowd.
A glass of cold Guinness was fetched, and Albert settled in a corner of the crowded snug, surrounded by eager faces.
"It was like this", said Albert, "In the early sixties; I think it was 1961, I was working at an engine shed in the Peak District. It was mostly freight work, but we 'ad a bit of passenger traffic as well. It was my job to relieve crews and dispose of locos after they'd come on shed at the end of a turn.
Well, we 'ad two fellas on that shed who was rum, to say the least. One was Jim Groggan, a driver known for making life 'ard for any fireman who 'e didn't 'appen to like, which was most of them. The other chap was Geoff Redhead. He was aptly named, in fact, hot head would have been more fitting, for 'e 'ad a hell of a temper on 'im. In fact, it were said that sometimes words 'ad come nearer to blows on one or two trips. Now, Geoff was a fireman.
The shed foreman dreaded the thought of these two getting together on the footplate, an' 'e did 'is best to ensure that their rosters kept them apart, but ultimately to no avail."
"Another Guinness, Albert?" called the barman.

12

"Aye!", chuckled Albert" This story-telling lark is thirsty work!"
All the regulars laughed as Albert got into his stride once more.

"Well, unfortunately, one fateful evening in late autumn, Bill, for that was the foreman's name, was really strapped for locomen. There'd been a flu epidemic thereabouts, and nearly 'alf of our reliefmen were off sick with it, so he was forced to call in Jim and Geoff to take out the 10.30 pm Derby unfitted freight.
Well, when the shed staff heard about the roster, they knew what was likely to 'appen. In fact, one of 'em, Terry (he worked down at the coaling stage), reckoned he was a bit psychic, and 'e turned up at Bill's office and said, 'It'll be the death of one or t'other of them, I'm telling thee. I think it'd be better to cancel Derby train than risk those two on the same footplate!'
How prophetic those words turned out to be!
However, Bill was 'aving none of it, and told Terry, 'I can't cancel the train 'cos of your daft ideas, now get out and get on with your own job.'

Anyroad, by now Jim Groggan had turned up and collected his things for the run, and after reading the latest route notices, he'd set off to the loco. It was a 4F 0-6-0, and it'd certainly seen better days. Well, before 'e'd even got on the footplate we could 'ear 'im chivelling at Geoff, but we shrugged our shoulders and got on with job in 'and.
Anyway, the freight got off twenty minutes down, so it

didn't bode well for the trip. In fact, they 'ad to stop
near Monsal Dale for a brew up, (that's what the locomen
call it when they have to stop to get steam up)."

At this point, Albert stopped to light his pipe, while the
crowd, by now much increased in size, pondered on their
new found knowledge of railway jargon.
"Come on, Albert, we haven't got all night!" said a young
lad at the back. With this, the old man took up the tale
once more.
"While they were stopped in the loop, Geoff 'ad gone up
into the signalbox to remind the bobby about their stay
in the loop; y'know like the rulebook says. It was obvious
that the engine was steaming badly, and according to
what Geoff said to the signalman, Jim Groggan put all
the blame squarely at Geoff's door.
Anyroad, Geoff cussed and swore about old Jim; the
upshot being that 'e wasn't taking much more on it, and
'e left the box with these fateful words 'It's the fire's
this an' it's the fire's that. If 'e says much more about
the fire, I'll put 'im on the ****** fire!'

With these words, Albert stopped for a drink, and,
perhaps to add to the dramatic effect, he mopped his
brow, before continuing.
"By now the freight was 70 minutes down, so it was no
surprise when the train passed the next signalbox at a
fair lick. What was more of a surprise was it rattling
through a 30 mph speed restriction at way over that.
Anyway, within minutes the signal 'train running away
right line' was being belled between boxes, for there was

14

nothing on that stretch of line that any of the signalmen could do to stop it. But they all knew where it would end if it didn't slow down.

Just near Rowsley there's a downgrade that finishes with a curve. Now normally, it's no problem, but the loco wa' flying by now, an' what with 500 tons of unfitted wagons pushing it, the train jumped the rails at this curve and ended up a wreck in the fields below."

'What happened to enginemen?' asked one of the curious bystanders, who was stood thoughtfully drinking his ale.

"Well, I was just coming to that, and you mustn't forget the guard on the rear of train too!" said Albert excitedly, as the gathering in the snug muttered amongst themselves, eagerly awaiting the outcome of this sad story.

"Of course there was an enquiry, an' it came out in th' wash that the guard, after doing all he could to attract the traincrew's attention, had pinned down his brake, and realising they weren't slowing, had jumped out a mile or two back. He had a broken leg and arm, but he thought himself lucky to be alive. They found Geoff's mangled body in a heap half way down the incline, next to a river."

"But what about the driver; I think you said his name was Groggan?" This was the voice of the barman, who by now had also become engrossed in the tale.

"Well, to tell you the truth, they never found his body." The crowd gasped, and all fell silent.

"Being the time o' year it was, the river where they found Geoff's body was in full flood, an' it was believed at the time that Jim must have jumped clear of the train, only to drown an' get washed away in the torrent."

"But...", by now those gathered were getting restless, and several voices seemed to utter this telling word.

Someone in the lounge was laughing, and calling for another beer. All Albert's audience shouted "Be quiet!", and with that, the offending voice, bemused by such a retort, faded into a murmur.

"Now we get to the REALLY interesting bit!" This was spoken slowly and deliberately by Albert, who knew by now that he had the assembled listeners hanging on his every word.

The room fell deadly silent, as Albert picked up the final threads of the tale.

"Any steam loco that disgraced itself by then was destined for scrap, and so it turned out. It was dragged back onto the track and sent for cutting up at Derby. Now I don't know if it's fate, or what, but I was made redundant a few days after the smash, and the railway, not wishing to part wi' the services of such a valuable employee...."

Everyone, including Albert laughed.

"Anyroad, I was what they called 'used to best advantage', which meant that they found me any work they could until another job in my grade came along. So fortune found me at Derby Works, just as the fateful loco took a final journey to its birthplace, an' it's place of decease, as it 'appened."

A final swig of beer was taken, and Albert put down his pipe, a sure sign that the story was coming to its grand finale.

"Engines weren't always cut up straight away at that

16

time, as there was such a backlog of withdrawn locos all over the place, an' it were a couple of months before we got to scrapping this engine. I had the job of dealing with the firebox, 'cos, I don't know if you know, but it's made of copper, so extra care was taken wi' it's salvage".

"Well, I remember the day I cut up that firebox. I won't forget it for the rest of me natural, I can tell you. It were pouring down, and the rest of the gang, who'd bin working on the smokebox an' tender, 'ad got soaked, so they went off to get changed. I carried on on me own. What the Health and Safety Committee would 'ave said, I can only guess!" he chuckled to himself. "I'd pulled out a few firebars, when the whole box keeled over. I jumped out of the way smartish, I can tell you, 'cos several ton of metal landing on you doesn't improve your health!"
"You might have been killed then Albert!"said the barman, and added jokingly "And we would have had some peace and quiet!"
The crowd in the snug exploded with laughter, but Albert, taking control again, said
"Aye, but I saw what I saw, all the same!"
The room fell silent once more.
Albert continued "Just before the firebox hit the floor, crushing everything under its weight, something fell out of it."
There was a gasp among the listeners; a sort of gasp of expectation, as if a veil was about to be lifted, but people weren't too sure they'd like what it would reveal.
Finally, someone in the room broke the chill with the inevitable -

"What?"

Albert hesitated, then in a rush of emotion that seemed to hark back to that river in flood all those years ago. "Charred bones!"

# MENTAL BLOCK

"Eighty pounds! Sold to the man in the blue jacket over there."

With that the hammer fell, and the lot was removed from the auctioneer's table to make way for the next item.

The money changed hands at the cashier's office a few minutes later, and Dave walked out onto the side street in the pouring rain a few minutes later with his new acquisition.

"A signalling block instrument for only eighty pounds!" chuckled Dave to himself, "and one with integral bell and tapper". He felt very lucky for once, because he'd heard tales of station 'totem' signs fetching hundreds of pounds, and steam loco nameplates, well, you didn't even dare think about them!

Dave had been suffering from depression a bit of late, so his wife, Pam, had suggested a day off work would do him good. When he mentioned he was going to the salerooms, Pam thought that was a grand idea, as at least he'd be with people.

"It's good to be with other folk", she said "It's doesn't do anyone any good to be on their own too much."

Pam was sensible like that, Dave thought, and so here he was, walking down his drive with a railway relic one Thursday in October, after a day at the sales.

"What you bought, love?" came Pam's voice across the kitchen as Dave struggled in with his large carrier bag.

"It's a block instrument" said Dave with pride.

"A what?" The reply was predictable, for Pam didn't share Dave's passion for things railway. "Anyway, here's a cup of tea, so you just get out of your wet things, then tell me how your day has gone."

With that, Dave trooped off into the hall, took off his coat, and returned a few minutes later with some cleaning cloths and tools.

"It's the signalman's stock in trade, so to speak", Dave said to Pam as he started to clean the casing. "You know, the thing that they tap out bell signals on and use to communicate with each other."

"Maybe I need one!" laughed Pam " 'Cos sometimes I reckon I'd do better using one of them 'block' things to get through to you than having a conversation! I always thought that railway enthusiasts used a different language to everyone else. Now I know it's true."

With that rebuke, Pam left Dave to his own devices, or to be more specific, to his own block instrument.

"I just don't understand it!" muttered Dave to no-one in particular. "I've tried all sorts to get this blasted thing to work, and still it won't tap out a bell code or give me a ring."

After bringing the contraption home, Dave had set about getting it to work, using batteries and voltmeters and all kinds of testing gear. He had a practical bent that way, but despite all his efforts, not a sound would come out of, or an indication come up on the recalcitrant device.

Plenty of sound came out of Pam however.

"Put that thing away, and get your tea!" came the cry

one evening.

"That thing will be the death of you, if you carry on chivelling away at it like you have been doing", shouted Pam from the kitchen "Or it'll be the death of me. Now get washed and get to the table."

With these words, Dave reluctantly gave up the quest for the Holy Bell Code for the night, and came sulkily to the kitchen table.

Not to be beaten, Dave continued to try ever more elaborate methods to get the block instrument to do its stuff. That is, communicate with sound via the bell and visually with the indicator needle.

To be honest, the project was starting to get him down, but he just couldn't seem to let go of this idea of communicating with someone, anyone, using an historic piece of signalling equipment.

Come December, there was still no luck with the temperamental gadget, so one afternoon, after a particularly frustrating session, Dave shouted upstairs to Pam, "I'm off up town for another multimeter, love, shan't be long!"

With that the door slammed and he was gone.

Pam finished getting changed and came down to the living room, where by now the block instrument had pride of place on the table, surrounded by wire and solder and God knows what.

"What a mess!" Pam muttered to herself "I'll be communicating wi' me tongue, never mind bell signals when he gets back!"

Pam turned her back on the infernal device, but just

then she heard two distinct rings behind her.

"What's that?"

At first she thought it must be the alarm clock, but then she said to herself "Don't be daft, the clock's not in here, and besides nobody sets an alarm clock for four o'clock in the afternoon. It must be that bell contraption."

With that, Pam spun round to look at it.

"Good Heavens!"

It wasn't just the sight of the bell, still vibrating, that brought this cry from her, but the needle in the indicator window.

It was pointing sharply to the right, into the red section marked 'Train on line'.

Perplexed, she sat down and swore that something was amiss here.

"I want that thing out of my house, and I'll tell Dave so when he gets back!" Pam thought out loud.

Soon after, there was a knock at the door.

"That'll be him!" Pam said to herself. "The daft beggar must have forgotten his keys."

With that she opened the door, but it was not a familiar face that confronted her. It was a policeman.

"Can I come in please?" asked the officer "I think it will be better if we talk inside."

The two of them walked to the living room, and sat down as best they could amongst the debris of her husband's endeavours. There was silence for a few moments, broken when Pam got up and said "Do you want a cup of...."

The officer politely interrupted "I think that you best stay seated." He continued after a short pause "I'm afraid

I have to inform you that your husband has been hit by
a train."
"Is he badly injured?" Pam whispered.
"I'm afraid that your husband was killed instantly. I'm
very sorry." There was a bigger pause, until Pam
summoned up the breath to say softly,
"How did it happen?"
"It appears that your husband took a short cut over the
railway line, down near the station level crossing.
Unfortunately, the Leeds train was just passing and he
was killed instantly where he stood in the middle of the
track."
"Then it was a terrible accident!" Pam interrupted.
"I'm afraid we can't be sure of that" the policeman
replied.
"The signalman saw him cut through the fence just
before the train arrived, and despite the signalman's
warnings, your husband appeared to just stop and stare
at the train."
The policeman continued "Of course there will be an
inquest, and until then, it has to be a matter of
conjecture."
After going through the formalities in such a situation,
and ensuring that Pam's neighbour would come round
to be with her, he got up to leave, when Pam stopped
him and said "At what time did it happen?"
The officer looked at his watch.
"Just over twenty minutes ago."
A shiver went up Pam's spine.
"Thank you. I'll let you out."
When he had gone, Pam looked again at the block

instrument. The needle was vertical.

The inquest came and went. 'Suicide while the balance of mind was disturbed' was the verdict, for the medical record of Dave's depression had come out, and coupled with the evidence of the driver and signalman, it seemed the only outcome.

Spring came, and as Pam started to pick her life up again she decided, as people do, to have a clear-out, but Dave's railway stuff was a problem.
"I'll call Uncle Bill. He'll know what it's worth, and what to do with it all."
Uncle Bill certainly did, for he sorted it out and advised Pam on all aspects of Dave's collection. However, when he got to the block instrument, he said something strange.
"Do you know where this came from?"
"The auction" Pam replied.
"No, I mean from which signalbox was it taken?" came Bill's reply.
"I don't know" she answered.
"Did he get this working?"
"Well no..... and yes" came Pam's cryptic reply, and with that the whole story came out, including the mysterious occurrence on the day of Dave's death.
"Ah" said Bill knowingly. Then he paused and seemed to dig deep in his memory for something that Pam could only guess at. After an interval of perhaps ten seconds, he continued.
"Many years ago, more than I care to remember, there

24

was an incident on the old Hull & Barnsley line near here."

"An incident?" Pam queried.

"Yes, an incident, or to be more specific, a suicide."

There was an ominous pause, which Pam broke with the universal appeal.

"Do you want a cup of tea, you know, before you tell me about it?"

"That would be nice" came Bill's response, thankful for a little space to gather his thoughts and tell the tale as tactfully as he could.

Pam returned shortly with the elixir of life and Bill once more picked up the thread of the story.

"Before the line shut in the 1950s, a signalman committed suicide at a signalbox in a deep cutting about ten miles from here. I think it occurred in the early hours of a December morning when the traffic was slack. In fact, it would have been slack", he mused to himself "For the line only had a few months to go before closure."

"How did he..." Pam paused "Do it, you know, kill himself?"

"That's the grotesque part. Apparently, he sent the ' train on line ' bell signal in both directions, turned the block instrument to the same, went down the steps and drowned himself in the water butt!"

There was a shocked silence, only broken when Pam asked "And what is a ' train on line ' signal?"

"Two rings on the bell, and a turn of the indicator needle to the right, into the red zone."

All was now becoming clear, or as clear as things can be

in such circumstances.

Almost immediately Pam screamed "I want that thing out of my house, Now!"

Bill had recognised the equipment as similar to that used on the line, but he couldn't be sure that it was from THAT box.

"I can understand how you feel, but this probably isn't one of the instruments in question."

"Yes it is. He was always obsessed with it, from the moment that he brought the damn thing in the house. Get it out of my sight!"

She would hear no more of the matter, and so Bill had to decide quickly what to do with the offending object.

"Wednesday" he said to himself "They'll be taking lots in at the auction for tomorrow's sale." With that he grabbed his hat, and put the block instrument in the car and drove down to the saleroom.


"Eighty five pounds!"

Down went the auctioneer's hammer "Sold to the chap in the anorak."

Pausing to pick up his tea, the salesman yelled to the lucky buyer,

"It's the end of the line for you!"

Everyone laughed, while the hapless buyer shambled off to collect his purchase and pay his dues.

Everyone that is, except an old man in a raincoat near the cashier's desk.

As the enthusiast left the saleroom at his moment of triumph, he heard behind him a sinister voice whisper ominously.....

"Another one for the block!"

# A QUESTION OF TIMING

"Come here you little! ....." The last words were lost in the autumn air, as Jason ran out of earshot, and into the night.

"Shan't go back" he muttered under his breath, as he stumbled down the lane that led to his friend Craig's house. Jason often had rows with his stepfather, but tonight's was by far the worst. He'd run out before, but he'd always returned, cowed, a little later. Things hadn't been easy since his mother died, and he spent as much time as possible in his bedroom reading. He loved to lose himself for hours at a time in pictures of the steam age.

"I'll teach him a lesson" he said defiantly to himself.

Engrossed in his childish anger, he turned a corner and knocked someone into a hedge.

"Watch yourself, stupid!" cried out the victim.

"Sorry, I wasn't looking where I was going" apologised Jason. Helping the boy out of the hedge, he said, with a look of surprise "Oh, it's you, Craig! What are you doing out at this time?"

"I was coming round to your house to look at your railway books" replied Craig "My parents were getting on my nerves. I just don't think they understand me."

"Better not come round to my place either then, Craig. Dad's mad at me, so I was thinking of teaching him a lesson by staying out all night."

With a glint in his eye, Craig said "Tell you what, Jason, let's both sleep out in the bushes. That'll teach our parents a lesson, and stir up this sleepy little place, won't it!"

So a plan started to take form among the chill mists of an October evening that was to change the way folk would remember their village forever. However, their juvenile reverie was soon shattered by the flash of headlights and the scream of a car approaching rapidly.
"Police!" yelled Craig, as he grabbed Jason and both fell backwards into a copse of trees.
"That was close!" exclaimed Jason, as the car sped past "What do we do now?"
Craig thought for a moment and said "We better make ourselves scarce."
"Good idea" replied Jason "But where?"
As they were quickly discovering, it's all very well to run away from something, but it helps to have a good idea of where you're running to. Home may seem like Hell, but as they were to discover, it is possible to go from the frying pan into the fire.

Craig, who was now getting up to speed with events, quickly responded "Down the embankment, in the railway cutting. We'll get chance to cop some of the night freights that we never get to see. I don't think the police will look there."
A five minute walk brought them to the over-bridge, and not a moment too soon, for as they scrambled down the embankment towards the tracks, another police car, with spotlight glaring, crawled over the bridge as they slithered down the muddy slope.
Holding their breath, they listened to the crunch of road

gravel, as the car slowly made its sweep of the area. After what seemed like an eternity, the sound receded and they were left with the distant rumble of an approaching passenger train.

"Close call!" shouted Jason as the train thundered past.

"Just another HST!" came Craig's obtuse reply "I hope we're going to see something more interesting if we're going to freeze ourselves to death train spotting."

Jason pulled a chocolate bar out of his jacket pocket. "Want a bit?"

"Sure" Craig replied. Biting into this delicacy, he continued "We might cop a few 66s if we can stay awake long enough."

"That would be alright, but I get fed up with watching diesels all the time" Jason mused.

Craig thought for a short while, and then became animated "Yeah, I know what you mean. Wouldn't it be great if we could slip back in time and watch this line in the steam days of the 50s, or better still, when the G.W.R. and L.M.S. fought it out along these lines!"

"Now, that would be something, Craig!" Jason replied in excitement.

With that, the conversation drifted to other things. The late hours became the small hours, and as the stream of traffic dwindled, sleep overtook both lads on that autumn night.

There's an old adage that says 'Be careful what you wish for – you may get it', and so it proved to be that night, when fate turned the two boys' dreams into nightmare. Jason woke to the singing of the rails. Shivering, he

30

dragged himself into the land of the living, rubbed his eyes and glanced at his watch. It was still dark, but dawn was fast approaching.

"Hey, wake up!" he said, as he tugged Craig's jacket. "It's just after five in the morning. Might as well get one or two more numbers before we return home like ghosts and scare everyone to death!"

"What?" mumbled Craig sleepily, before he commented curiously "What's that sound I can hear?"

"A train, of course!" said Jason laughing. "Remember, we fell asleep on the embankment next to the railway." Craig, who was now waking up rapidly, responded excitedly "But surely that's the sound of a steamer on the up line?"

A perplexed look crossed both faces as the unmistakable bark of a steam exhaust filtered through the foggy morning air.

Jason and Craig leapt to their feet and staggered down the last few feet into the cutting, to be greeted by a sight they would remember for the rest of their lives.

"Craig, am I dreaming this?" Jason shouted.

Wide-eyed, Craig replied "No, I can see it too!"

Staring in total disbelief, they looked one way and saw an old L.M.S. engine on a freight train as it gradually rattled towards where they were standing under the road-bridge.

However, it was the spectacle in the opposite direction that caused their eyes to leap out of their sockets. For there, storming out of the swirling mist and over-running the home signal at danger, came a mail train,

31

headed by another L.M.S. steam loco. Blocking the line in front of the mail train was a freight setting back into sidings, propelled by an engine that was unmistakably of G.W.R. origin.

The fast mail train hit the G.W.R. train and ricocheted across the tracks, into the path of the lumbering freight. It then cut the string of wagons of the up freight in two, and hurtled towards the two lads.

"Oh my God, wake up!" flashed through Jason's terrified mind.

Frozen to the spot, Craig screamed "This would be a good time to wake up!"

The two boys never returned home. Despite an extensive search, no trace was ever found of them. How could two youngsters just disappear off the face of the earth? How, indeed.

And so the name of Charfield became associated doubly with tragedy. On the morning of October 13th 1928, fifteen lives were lost in a collision which involved the 10pm Leeds to Bristol passenger and parcels train, the 9.15pm Oxley Sidings to Bristol fitted goods, and the 4.45am Westerleigh to Gloucester empty freight. The coaches following the L.M.S. train from Leeds piled up against the bridge and immediately burst into flames fuelled by escaping gas. Despite brave efforts by all attending the accident, it was twelve hours before the blaze was extinguished.

The line was cleared, an inquiry was held, the dead were buried, but one mystery remained for the investigators - who were the two children found in the wreckage, burned beyond recognition? No one claimed them. No one missed them. Who would let their children travel overnight unaccompanied?

Who indeed, one could ask, for no one came forward to provide the answer.

In Charfield graveyard, in an unnamed grave, lie the mortal remains of the only two people who could tell the tale of that star-crossed October morning. So the twenty-first century gained a tragedy and the twentieth century, a mystery.

Had they lived, what a story they would have had to tell, for as they found out, there is a fine line between dream and disaster.

It's all a question of timing.

# GHOST RIDER

"We'll be away as soon as I get my billycan filled with tea. I'll give you the all clear as soon as I get back."
With that, Arthur Smith, our rider, crunched down the cinder track to the messroom for his brew.

These were sad days, for many of the locomotives that we'd worked on, cussed, and sometimes loved, were now going to the scrapyard. That's the way things go, call it modernisation, but we all knew in the back of our minds that our jobs could be following these engines soon.

My fireman for the trip, Harry, climbed onto our engine, a 'Black Five', and throwing his bag onto the footplate, said "You alright, Sid? Always a bit sad when we have to take these old 'uns to the knacker's yard."

"You're right there. We've three to take today. I see we've got old 56, Wilf Fraser's engine."

With that, I checked the gauges, and my mind meandered off down a pleasant path to think of Wilf and his favourite pilot engine - 56. She was an 0-6-0 tank, often called a 'Jinty', and was used on runs between the local sidings, the station and the depot. It had been Wilf's loco for as long as most folk could remember. He'd grown attached to the dirty old thing, and being a bit of a wag, he'd had the brass letters '56' attached to his engineman's cap, which he wore with pride. Engines had five figure numbers, but at the shed, most railwaymen just referred to the last two or three.

"Where's Arthur? The foreman said he was to be our rider today."

34

Harry's words brought me back to earth "Oh yes, he's our man. He'll give us the all clear when he gets back from the bothy in a minute" I replied.

Now a rider is someone who rides on the rear dead loco of a train consisting of scrap locomotives. Without steam, the engines in our train had no brakes, and so an experienced man had to keep a look out at the back, and apply the handbrake if required. An example would be if a coupling snapped, and the train became divided.

Harry continued "Fire's a bit dirty, but I don't think we'll have any problems wi' this trip". He paused, leaned on the fire iron and added "Did you hear, Sid, Wilf retired the same day that his loco was withdrawn last month. Don't you think that's uncanny?"

"Aye, so I heard" I replied noncommittally.

With that Harry chuckled to himself, and I leaned out of the cabside and looked in the direction of the end loco in our doomed entourage.

"That's the all clear, Arthur's just given me the hand signal from the cab of 56".

"OK" replied Harry.

With that, I glanced to check that the release road signal was off. It was, and so I eased the handbrake off and opened the regulator. There was a moment's hesitation before the 'Black Five' responded, but then we were off.

We could hear the dead locos protesting behind us, as the tired wheels and even tireder bearings carried these once proud steamers to their final resting place. Smoke drifted lazily past the cab window, as our sombre cavalcade rumbled along. Even on that short journey, we were to pass several signalboxes. The expressions on the faces of the signalmen gave away how they felt. We felt it too. It was the end of the line in so many ways for the life we'd known. The steam locomotive was passing, and most railwaymen held an inner sadness for what that represented.

Within the hour we were at the scrapyard. We eased into the reception road like an interloper at someone's funeral. Bits of loco parts were heaped around us like some macabre mechanical slaughterhouse. The 'Black Five' had hardly wheezed to a halt when the yard foreman ran up and said "You better ring the depot straight away. There's been some kind of mix-up."
I leapt off our engine, leaving the warmth of the cab of my living engine to face the winter winds as I walked the short distance to the office. Once inside, I warmed my hands in front of the roaring coal fire. There was never any shortage of coal here, for there was always loads off the bunkers and tenders of the recently departed. To many, the removal of coal from a condemned engine was like the last rites to the dying.
I picked up the telephone and said assuredly "Sid here. You wanted to speak to me."

I was a lot less assured when I walked back to Harry on the engine five minutes later.
"What's up?" asked Harry, seeing I was troubled.
"Come with me down the line to 56."
"Why?" came Harry's reply.
"It seems we left Arthur behind at the depot."

36

"You what! You saw him give you the wave, didn't you?"
Harry probably thought that I was having him on.
"I'm sure I saw him give me the sign. Anyway, I
definitely saw someone on the rear loco wave the all
clear to me."
By this time, we were alongside the cab of 56. We climbed
up the stone cold cabside, half expecting to see Arthur
miraculously appear on the cramped footplate.
There was no Arthur. There was his duty bag and pack-
up, but no sign of the man. However, what did catch our
attention was the dirty grease-cloth cap on the driver's
seat.
"That's Wilf's cap!" exclaimed Harry "It can't be, but it
is. Tell me if I'm wrong, Sid."
Sure enough, the old battered hat bore the gleaming
letters 56 on them. There was no mistaking Wilf's old
cap.
I said solemnly "We'll see what the foreman has to say
when we get back to the depot as light engine. Let's pick
up the cap and take Arthur's gear back with us."
With that, we climbed down the loco steps and with
heavy hearts, we trudged back in the icy drizzle to our
engine.

Within forty minutes our loco rolled into the depot yard,
and I stepped down with Arthur's stuff and our strange
offering. Once in the running foreman's office, our heads
were on the block.
"What the hell do you think you were doing, leaving
the depot without your rider behind. You don't need me
to tell you the possible consequences if there'd been a

problem, you're both experienced men!"

Andy, the shift foremen was really laying it on.

Harry leapt in "Sid says he was given the all clear. I didn't see it myself, but I trust Sid's judgement"

Leaning back in his chair, Arthur butted in "How could I give you the nod, when I was talking to the lads in the messroom as you left?"

Speaking softly, I lifted my head and uttered "I don't know, but someone did, and I'm wondering if it's the same someone who left Wilf Fraser's hat on the driver's seat of his old engine."

With that, I flicked the cap onto the running foreman's desk.

Andy jumped up from his chair "What the hell!"

After a moment's pause, Arthur stepped from his chair, and carefully examining the hat declared "Yes, that's Wilf's old cap alright."

Andy had regained his composure now, and taking charge of the situation said "Wilf always was one for a lark. It's just possible he's having a bit of a laugh at our expense, especially seeing it was his loco that went to the scrapyard today. I'll 'phone him at home and see what he's up to".

We waited patiently as Andy dialled Wilf's home. However, far from clarifying the situation, the conversation that followed left all in the foreman's office bewildered. We could only grasp snatches of the words spoken from the other end, and we all tried to guess what the perplexed expressions on the foreman's face could mean. After a few minutes, Andy slowly put the receiver down. He seemed shocked and puzzled.

"Wilf passed away today" After a pause, Andy continued "That was his sister. She went round to Wilf's house earlier when he didn't answer the phone. She has a key, and when she went in, she found him slumped over the kitchen table, with his railway photographs laid out before him".

An eerie calm fell in the office.

The sound of live steam shattered the dead silence surrounding us, and brought us back to our senses again. It was only an engine blowing off steam on the coaling road.

Harry said solemnly "I wonder when the funeral will be? I'm sure a lot of the lads would want to pay their last respects".

"Aye, that's right" piped up Arthur.

Being the pragmatist, I pointed to the deceased driver's cap on the desk and remarked "Well, that puts paid to any theory about Wilf playing practical jokes today."

"Well, it's a mystery all the same, and I'll have to put a report in" Andy said thoughtfully, before continuing "I hope we haven't got a joker who's going to start playing tricks that threaten safe running around here."

Indeed, it seemed we hadn't got a serial trickster, for no further reports of malpractice were received in the coming days. Wilf's funeral was scheduled for the following Friday afternoon. I was rostered for the early shift that day, and as luck would have it, I passed the scrapyard that morning. As we drifted by on a fitted freight, I noticed that the cutters had just started on

Wilf's loco. Their torches had made inroads into the front buffer-beam and one side tank. Somehow, it seemed appropriate that 56's demise should proceed on that day.

It was a dismal afternoon that saw forty railwayman gathered round the graveside to pay our last respects to our former colleague. Through the thin rain, Wilf's son, John, walked up to me as I watched the last stragglers leaving the graveyard.

"Sid, I understand that you've got Dad's old cap."

"That's right, it's at home. I thought of bringing it along, but there's not even a gravestone to put it on yet."

John chose his words carefully and then continued "It would mean a lot to me if I could have Dad's hat. It was like his trademark."

Putting my trilby back on, I replied "That's no problem. It should go to his next of kin. Come with me, we'll pick it up off my sideboard now."

With that, John and I stepped away from Wilf's last resting place and down streets that seemed to have faded to grey.

"Where the hell has it gone!" I exclaimed after the third search of my home.

"Are you sure you didn't leave it at work?" replied John, trying to placate me.

"No, I damn well didn't. It has to be here somewhere!"

But it wasn't, for a fourth search proved equally fruitless. It was with some concern that I bade John farewell, and promised him that I would forward the wayward item, should it appear.

The following week I was rostered to take two more scrap engines to the yard. While at the yard, I took the opportunity to inspect old 56. All that remained were the driving wheels laid out at either side of the breaker's main road. I spotted the works plate for 56 among the debris next to the acetylene bottles. Picking it up, I rubbed it to a rough sheen as I strode to the foreman's office. It was lunch time, and he was biting heartily into a bacon sandwich as I walked in.

"How much do you want for this?" I enquired, as the foreman took a swig of his tea.

"Give us five bob" he spluttered as he started on his grub again.

"Fine" I said, and with that I put two half crowns on the desk, picked up my trophy and walked out.

I was due off at one o'clock that afternoon. I had a crazy idea of visiting Wilf's grave that day and showing him the plate. The sun was shining as I swung open the cemetery gates and stepped towards it. Behind me, I heard the creak of the gates again, and glancing round, I saw John striding towards me.

"Hello Sid. Nice to see you, I come here every day just to talk to Dad. I know it seems daft, but it stops me missing him so bad."

As we walked on, John asked tentatively "Did you find Dad's old cap?"

With some trepidation, I replied gently "No, no trace whatever. I even looked at work, but it's nowhere to be found". Changing tack, I pulled out the works plate from my coat pocket and continued "But, I did recover this from Wilf's old loco and brought it along today for old time's sake."

"That's nice" John chirped up as we turned down the last gravel path to Wilf's graveside.

Nothing could prepare us for the sight that met us, for there on the freshly heaped earth was Wilf's old driver's cap!

"What an earth!" exclaimed John, staggering up to the mound before adding "I swear it wasn't there yesterday!" as he gently lifted the well worn memento.

Stunned, I struggled for words, before muttering "None of this makes any sense, but they say that there's more things in heaven and earth."

With that, I laid the metal plate down respectfully next to the cloth cap. John and I stared across the tombstones for what seemed an eternity at the setting sun. Then, without exchanging any words, we both turned and walked away, leaving the dying rays to merge the gleam of brass and steel into a shimmering rail leading skywards, guiding man and machine to their ultimate destination.

# THE DREWTON TUNNEL POSSESSION

"Here's a story that I haven't told anyone before, because no one would have ever believed it."

These words were spoken by my Uncle Jack, just before he died. He had worked for many years on the former Hull & Barnsley Railway, mostly as a trackman. I'd spent many a happy evening listening to his tales of the steam years, and so my ears pricked up with this revelation.

"What's that, Uncle?" I replied.

"No one's heard this story. We were told to hush it up, it being in the darkest days of the last war. Security an' all that, you know. Thought it might have a bad effect on British morale."

"What are you talking about? Let's hear it then!" I said eagerly.

My Uncle Jack propped himself up in his bed and began to recall the strange tale that I now pass on to you.

"It was December 1941, and at that time I was employed on the L.N.E.R. as a platelayer, maintaining the track. Now my patch was the South Cave to Little Weighton length, which included Drewton Tunnel. It was over a mile long, and as nasty to walk as any tunnel, but I never had any reason to fear it. Not until that night......"

With that he seemed to gaze into the distance, through the walls and to some distant place.

"What night, Uncle?"

43

"Well, the down track needed relaying because a combination of heavy war traffic, mostly coal, and damp conditions in the tunnel had made it wear badly, so we took possession of the tunnel."

"You what!" I'd never heard this expression before, even though Uncle Jack had talked about his job often before. "What do you mean – you took possession?"

"The Engineer's Department, that is the Civil Engineer's, although they weren't always civil!"

With that he laughed loudly before continuing, "They take over control of the line so that they can carry out essential work. We call it taking possession of the line. Anyway, the Engineers had taken possession of Drewton Tunnel that night, and after the P.I.C., that is, 'The Person in Charge', had informed us that both up and down tracks were blocked, and we were O.K. to start work, we walked into the tunnel. When I say we, there were a number of men involved, but I remember clearly Bob Hastings and Brian Waudby, as they were my mates.

Well, we'd taken some of the down rails out when Bob, who was about twenty feet from me said"

'Can you hear that, Jack?'

"Hear what?" I replied.

'There's a train coming along the up line. Can't you hear it?'

My uncle broke off to cough, then turned to me and continued "There was a note of panic in his voice, I could tell. Anyway, Bob didn't stop there, because then he called out 'Let's get out of here or we'll be killed!'

I thought he was having a funny turn, so I said 'Don't

44

be daft Bob, there's no train coming on either road. Remember, we've taken control of BOTH roads. Can you hear owt, Brian?"

Well, Brian was a bit off to my right, an' he shouted back 'No, he must be hearing things. Listened to too many air-raid sirens I reckon. Pull yoursen together, Bob!'

"With that, Bob raced past us like a man possessed, screaming 'Get out, get out, we'll all be killed.' I've never seen a face so full of terror, I can tell you."

"He'd gone mad, then", I said.

"Well you'd have thought so, an' that's what all the gang must have been thinking, 'cos he didn't run towards the mouth of the tunnel, as you'd expect, an' safety. He ran further INTO the tunnel, and pitch darkness!"

"What happened to him then?" I asked, as the tragedy unfolded.

"You may well ask that" my Uncle replied, and then said "We never found him."

I was baffled for a moment.

"He must have turned up somewhere."

"Well, we didn't find him that night, and he never returned home, not that night, or ever again."

"Maybe he ran for miles and then got struck by a train when the line re-opened" I replied, by now somewhat perplexed.

There was a pause, and then my Uncle Jack continued, sometimes struggling with the words.

"There was an enquiry, which didn't shed much light on it all, but what did come out was that there HAD

45

been a previous accident in Drewton Tunnel - in 1909. It was under similar conditions, but they were only operating single line working. That is, trains could come through the tunnel, even when men were working on 'tother track. It appears that an engine running wrong line struck a gang an' killed one of 'em. It was because of yon accident that we had possession of both tracks in 1941."

"So no one found out what happened to your mate - what was his name?"

"Bob Hastings", my uncle replied, turning white and suddenly looking old and fragile.

He then continued "Well, you can make of this what you like, but a few months after his disappearance, they found a body, badly mutilated, as if hit by a train, near the entrance to the tunnel. It could have been Bob."

"So it was as I said. He ran for miles and then was knocked down while his mind was still disturbed." I knew it was a bit feeble, but that was all I could find to say.

"Aye, you'd think so," came my uncle's reply "Funny part was the clothes he was wearing."

The story was anything but funny and so I rose to the bait.

"What do you mean - funny?"

There was a pause, and then my uncle, looking me straight in the eye, said in a voice cracking with emotion - "They were the working clothes of a Hull & Barnsley railwayman at the turn the century!"

# TRAILING CROSSOVER

"What a way to make a living, and on my birthday too!" muttered Dave to no one in particular. In fact, there was no one to mutter to, for he was, as usual, alone as he drove his delivery van.

What had brought the sudden outburst on from Dave was the start of a heavy downpour. Driving long distances in the middle of the night was bad enough, but ploughing through torrential rain seemed to increase the isolation. It really did make you feel like you were the only person awake in the country.

Turning the radio on, he cheered up a little.

"Mustn't grumble" he thought to himself. He felt that he'd been lucky to get the express delivery job with Top Link Services. The money wasn't bad, but the downside was the unsocial hours.

He knew this stretch of road well, the A19 from Selby to York. It always struck him as a particularly boring bit of asphalt, especially at three in the morning, but not this night.

"What the hell!"

For perhaps twenty seconds, Dave had watched the two faint lights getting closer, thinking they belonged to some fool driving his car on side lights. What was hurtling towards him now, at a distance of no more than three hundred yards was anything but that.

Beyond the hypnotising sway of the wipers, and through the haze of the driving rain, he was confronted by a locomotive bearing down on him at speed. There could be no mistaking the front end of an express steam engine, with the gleam of the two front lamps above the buffer beam. His headlights now picked up the glint of burnished buffers, and wheel flange against rail. With the ghostlike whiteness of the exhaust confronting him, ready to overwhelm his vehicle, Dave hit the brakes.

Just then, a cascade of sparks flew from either side of the locomotive.

"Oh God!" he yelled.

It felt as though his eardrums would burst, as a crescendo forged of steel and fire engulfed his vehicle. All the colours of the rainbow seemed to flash before his eyes, then all fell still.

Lifting his head a few moments later, all Dave saw was the dead hand of the wipers, going back and forth robotically as though nothing had happened. With no other vehicle in sight, the cat's eyes, wet with rain, glistened in the van's headlights.

Was he dead? No, he could still hear the faint judder as rubber on glass reverberated through the windscreen. Anyway, if it was Heaven, or even Hell, it looked suspiciously like the A19 on a wet night.

For some reason the radio was silent, so Dave turned it on again. The saccharine strains of some DJ came reassuringly across the airwaves.

Despite the inclement weather, Dave stepped out of the van, and putting both hands on the bonnet, he took a deep breath. Perhaps he'd dreamed it.

"A bit too vivid for me" he said under his breath.

The rain showed no mercy, descending relentlessly on the back of his aching head.

After a minute in the cold and rain, he came round a bit. He ran his hand through his hair, feeling the drops fall on his shirt. This was how it should feel, he thought. "Better get on."

Opening the driver's door, Dave sat down and gripped the driving wheel hard. He was brought back to his senses by a screech of brakes and the sound of a lorry's horn behind him.

"Damn!" He uttered, as he realised he was stopped right in the centre of the highway. Engaging first gear, he pulled over to one side and let the H.G.V. scream past.

Setting off again, the routine drive to Newcastle no longer seemed routine anymore as he had time to reflect on a night that was to change his life forever.


"Happy 50th birthday!" greeted Dave as he opened the door on his arrival back home at midday. The welcome came from his wife, Pat, who was sitting at the table supping tea with Dave's aunt, Irene.

Instinctively, his aunt could tell that something was amiss, and with concern in her frail voice, she said "What's troubling you, David? Had a near miss, or is there a problem at work?"

The driver was reluctant to speak, but gathering his thoughts, he replied "Actually, it could be a bit of both."

Two voices spoke as one "What do you mean?"

He sat down, poured a mug of tea, and leaning forward and resting his elbows on the table, he recited the events on the A19 just north of Selby early that morning.

"I can tell you, it fair shook me up!"

Worried, Pat replied "I'm not surprised, but what does it mean? Trains don't appear from nowhere, and definitely not on roads. There's no railway at Ricall, so how could you see a train! And anyway, you've driven that stretch of road countless times before and nowt's happened. I know it's your birthday, but why should it happen today, of all days?"

The three souls gathered in the room, staring at each other, pondered this for a few moments.

Aunt Irene suddenly became thoughtful, as though a long lost memory had just raised a flicker in her mind. "What's up, aunt?" asked Pat.

"I don't feel too well, so I think I'll get on home while it is still light".

Both Dave and Pat thought this a bit sudden, but Irene could be very determined, as only old folks can. She made her excuses and let herself out, and headed for the bus stop with one clear purpose in mind.

From that day, Dave's interests changed completely. Gone were the football and darts, and in was an almost obsessive fascination with railways, and steam locos in particular. He even told Pat that he'd started to dream about railways, and one in particular kept recurring. He was on the footplate of an express steam loco, it was dark and he was driving. He looked out into the driving rain, saw lights approaching, then all went black, and he would wake up in a state of panic.

"What does it mean?" asked the baffled van driver, to which Pat, shrugging her shoulders, obviously had no

50

answer.

Books on railways were borrowed from the library. He soon learnt to recognise different types of loco from publications that he bought on the internet. For some reason, his favourites were the Gresley A4 Pacifics, and he developed an ambition to drive one, perhaps at the North Yorkshire Moors railway. It was while poring over one of their leaflets about driving courses that he recognised the identity of the loco in his dream, and the one that had also confronted him on that lonely stretch of the A19 one winter's night. There on the front of the brochure was 'Sir Nigel Gresley', resplendent in blue livery.

"That's it, but in green!" he exclaimed to the budgie, chirping in the cage beside the living room table.

But neither he nor the budgie were any the wiser what it all meant.

"Fourteen on tonight", yelled the guard to Len, who had just stepped onto the footplate of 'Sir Nigel Gresley' at the head of the Kings Cross sleeper at Newcastle Central. With his fireman, Harry, they were rostered to take the heavy train down to London, and she was already twenty minutes down.

Len Shipley had been a top link driver for over ten years, and was familiar with Gresley's racehorses, the A4s. This one was a 'Top Shed' loco, and hadn't been out of works long, but the live steam injector was already proving temperamental, and Harry had spoken words to the effect that the fire wasn't up to much.

"Hope we get a clear run, Len" said Harry as he filled

the back corners of the firebox with coal.

With that, the signals came off, and with his experienced hand firmly on the regulator, Len eased it open, and felt the loco strain as it got to grips with over four hundred tons behind the tender. Surefootedly, the A4 crept out of the station and into the night, with two hundred and sixty eight miles to the Capital.

The engine responded well, and five minutes had been gained by Darlington. The long stop there gave Harry chance to get the fire more to his liking, and then it was off on the racing ground to York, forty four miles away. Glancing out at the clear signals on the fast road ahead, Len called across to his mate "We might just get a clear run! What do you reckon - ten minutes back leaving York?"

Harry laughed, and upon checking the gauge glasses, he said "You're an optimist!" and pointed a warning finger at one of them.

For Len had spoken too soon. Passing Northallerton, the troublesome injector had started its tricks again.

"Damn, just when we were doing so well!" Len muttered. Both looked at the offending water gauge, conscious that in a minute or two, the water happily bobbing around in the glass could be an inch or two lower. 60007 was steaming well, but not enough water was getting into the boiler.

As Thirsk station flashed past, Len edged the regulator back a touch to save on steam. Even so, the water level was near the bottom nut in the glass as the sleeper rolled into York just after two in the morning.

"Is there a fitter handy?" called Len as an inspector strode up the cab of 'Sir Nigel Gresley'.

"Only if you can wait ten minutes until we get one from the shed", came the reply.

Glancing at his watch, Len was acutely conscious that they were now twenty five minutes down. Should he fail the engine? It went against the grain for him, for he'd never had to declare a loco a failure since he'd been in the top link of drivers. That would be bad luck, he thought.

"I've got it going" cried Harry "Sweet as a nut". While Len had been talking to the chap on the station, Harry had performed a little black magic peculiar to injectors. Len leant across the cab, and sure enough, the level in the glass was rising and there was the kind of gurgling coming from the injector that was a mystery to layman, but would bring a smile to any engineman.

"What's it to be then?" called the inspector from the platform.

Len hesitated, then leaning out of the cab, he said purposefully "We'll risk it".

Station duties completed, the guard blew his whistle, and under clear signals, 60007 slid out of York with a full head of steam and a rising water level.

But that night, fate was to play cruel tricks with Len and Harry. No sooner had they passed Chaloner's Whin Junction, than the live steam injector gave up the ghost altogether.

"Harry, work some more of that magic over that damn thing!" yelled Len as he quickly gave a passing glance at the road ahead.

Worse was soon to follow, for the exhaust steam injector, a stalwart up 'till now, hesitated and fell silent. On top of that, a hard dull rain had started to fall.

"Oh no, we'll be dead by Selby unless we can get these devils working!" uttered Len in desperation.

60007 was still steaming well, and with a clear road ahead, both men turned their attention, albeit for a short time, to the miscreant mechanisms on the bulkhead.

When Len next looked out, he could scarce believe the sight in front of the train.

Gone was the familiar glint of steel rails, the comforting glow of signals in the distance, and in its place was a totally unfamiliar horizon.

Sure enough, it was still dark, it was still pouring with rain, and steam was streaming over the cab from a willing L.N.E.R. boiler. However, in the path of the loco, not a quarter of a mile away, was what looked like a set of car headlights driving straight at them.

"Do you see that!" screamed the startled driver to his mate.

Harry leapt to his window and stared forward. "See what? There's lights on at the crossing keeper's cottage, so someone's up very late. Is that what you mean?"

"No, there's a car on the track!" screamed Len in a panic.

Harry looked out again, and seeing nothing untoward, he turned round, and was met by a sight that would scare the living daylights out of any railwayman, for his mate was lying face down on the footplate.

"Len, Len, can you hear me!" yelled the anxious fireman. There was no response from the stricken driver, and

Harry had no choice but to bring the train to a stand in Selby station at just after three.

An ambulance was called, and Len was taken to hospital. The loco was declared a failure, and the passengers had to wait until another engine arrived from York depot for them to continue their journey southwards.

Harry now had time to kill, and while waiting in the station master's office, he called the hospital. After a few moments, his face turned ashen white.

"What's up, mate?" asked a duty porter who had just looked in.

"My mate, he's dead. Was already dead when he went into the ambulance" mumbled Harry quietly.

The porter hesitated, then walked over to the distraught fireman, who by now was slumped in a chair next to the desk, and said sympathetically "Dear, oh dear, what happened, mate?"

Harry, lifted his head, which had been in his hands, and replied "Look's like a massive heart attack, maybe brought on by shock they say, but it's early days yet to know for sure."

Puzzled, the Selby railwayman continued "I know the loco was a failure, but I wouldn't have thought that was much of a shock for a bloke."

Looking up, Harry replied "No, but before he collapsed, he was yelling about seeing a car on the track in front of us, about three miles north of here. I could see nothing, but next thing I knew, he was on the deck."

"Well, that must have been over an hour ago, so I reckon if owt was amiss on the line to York, we'd 'ave heard by now. Anyway, I'll pass that on to the inspector. I'm sure that they'll check it out" said the porter, as he stepped out of the door and onto the platform as an express goods rattled past on the down line.

Once on his own, Harry respectfully paid a final compliment to his former pal "At least he never failed a loco while he was a top link driver."

He then looked with sadness around the cluttered office, and glancing at the 1961 winter timetable on the wall, he muttered "December 14th, Len would have been fifty today."

One evening, a few weeks after Dave's birthday, Irene knocked at the door, and he let her in.

"I hope that you're feeling a lot better than last time. What brings you round – more birthday cake?"

They both laughed, and sitting down, Irene said resolutely "You said that the incident in the van happened just north of Selby. You know that your parents separated not long after you were born, and you were brought up by your grandparents in Leeds?"

Dave nodded in agreement, as he closed the book on the history of the L.N.E.R. lying on the table.

Irene then pulled out an old newspaper.

"What's that, a piece of your history?" Dave said with a chuckle.

Irene smiled, before opening with "No, I believe it is a piece of your history", with the emphasis on 'your'.

"How come?"

"I kept a York newspaper from the day you were born. It took me a while to find it, but here it is."

Opening the browned and creased sheets at page 10, she directed Dave's attention to an article entitled 'Driver drops dead on night train'.

Baffled, Dave replied "What's that to do with me?"

"Read on" said the aunt in an authoritative voice.

After a minute, Dave's face became thoughtful.

Irene continued "Remember that Pat said there was no railway line through Ricall? Well, as you have just read, there was fifty years ago - it was the main line to London from York. I remember that they diverted the main line and built the A19 on top of the old track north of Selby."

Baffled, Dave replied "So?"

"What your grandparents didn't tell you was that you were born at a railway crossing keeper's house near Ricall. At precisely three o'clock in the morning, on December 14th 1961 - exactly the time that the driver died, on the date of his 50th birthday!"

# THE PARLIAMENTARY

"You're mad!"
So said all the regulars at the Station Inn when Stanley
Ackroyd said he was going to catch THE train next
Friday.
"No one catches THE train anymore!" said Jim, a mate
of Stanley's "Anyroad, not that I know."
Having retired over twenty years earlier from a working
life spent entirely on the railway, Stanley felt a need to
catch the train once more, even though he wasn't as
sprightly as he used to be.
"A sort of solidarity thing", he said to himself "and for
old times sake too."
"Stan, I reckon you'll pop your clogs if they ever shut
that station" said Harry, the landlord "You've got
railways in the blood!" He filled Stan's glass once more.

The service from the local station had been reduced over
the years to just one commuter train that called once a
week, on Friday evening, taking any would be passengers
to town. It only really called now for statutory purposes
to keep the station open. The timing, 17.22, harked right
back to pre-grouping days, when the railway companies
were obliged to provide one 'stops all stations' service for
the benefit of all comers. In those far off days they
called it 'The Parliamentary', because it was provided
to fulfil the letter of the law, rather than out of any
commercial consideration by the railway companies
concerned.

It was early in December, in those dreary days that big stores say are Christmas, and normal people say are just plain cold and dark.

"Not the best time of year to travel" thought Stan to himself, but he'd said that he'd do it, and so he damn well was going to do it!

The following Friday, Stan had second thoughts, but he was a stubborn bloke. He left home in good time for the 17.22. The last rays of what passed for sunshine at this time of year had given up the ghost an hour earlier, and a thin drizzle accompanied him to the station.

'17.22' he thought to himself. In his day it would have been 5.22 pm, thank you!

He hadn't felt too well that day, and though he lived close to the station, he was quite tired by the time he walked onto the platform. In fact, he felt a bit foolish as well about his outing.

"Aye, and a bit down too" he thought, as he looked around the lonely halt on which he found himself. The station buildings had long gone, after being vandalised. Even the shelter and most of the lighting built to replace them had been vandalised too.

Stan was alone in this twilight world of semi-darkness. However, he had little time to take in his depressing surroundings, for on the wind he heard the sound of a train.

"That's unusual" he muttered to no-one "It's on time."

What was more unusual, he realised seconds later, was the sound.

"It's a steam loco, and steaming badly by the sound of it" he said to the still cold air. Must be one of those preserved locomotives that enthusiasts like to do up."

Aye, you had to be enthusiastic to tackle that, as he well knew. Fifty years on the railways had taught him how hard it could be "Anyroad" he mumbled to himself "It's a queer time of year to be running a special."
By the time these thoughts had run through his mind, the engine had appeared under the bridge and rumbled into the halt.
"If it is a preserved loco" he thought to himself "They've made a damn poor job of it!"
Indeed, the engine was so dirty that neither smokebox or cab number could be made out. The only 'livery', if you could call it that, was of lime streaks down the boiler and onto the discoloured side tanks.
However, Stan recognised the loco as what trainspotters used to call a C13 tank, an ex-G.C.R. type that he'd worked on many times in his prime.
"Didn't think any of these had been preserved!" he said to the driver, who gave him a knowing look.
At that moment, a carriage door opened and a welcoming light beamed out onto the dreary platform where Stan was standing.
"We've been expecting you!" said a voice familiar to Stan.
Glancing up, Stan saw the smiling face belonged to Jack Hartley. He'd worked many a shift with Jack, and the sight made Stan feel suddenly better.
"Hullo Jack" said Stan as he boarded the train, which seemed much fuller than he'd have thought on such a

dismal evening.

"Haven't seen you in a while. Last I heard you'd been badly."

" No, I'm fine now" said Jack in a hearty reply, as Stan took a seat near the window.

"Is that you Stan?" called out another voice from across the carriage.

It was Joe Ramsbottom, who as a foreman had always been good to Stan, especially in the way of a bit of overtime when money was tight.

Stan's earlier misgivings faded, and as he looked out into the chill night, he leant back contentedly in the seat and said to Joe, who had by now come down to sit next to him.

"I think it were a grand idea of mine to catch this train tonight. I wouldn't have missed it for dear life!"

Joe and Jack, and a few other familiar figures who had by now taken seats nearby, laughed, and Jack said "Aye, you're right there!"

As the irregular beat of the old loco gathered speed, Stan felt at home.


A maintenance man found Stan's body next morning on the platform, and it was a sombre crowd who gathered at the Station Inn that night.

"They say they found his body under a sign announcing the closure of the station" said Harry "I told him the shock would kill him!"

"I'm surprised he could see it down there at that time, what with the lights the way they are" said Pete, a railwayman himself, and another steady customer at the pub.

Jim looked over his glass and gasped "So he didn't catch the train after all then."

"Obviously he didn't!" boomed Harry "Any more drinks, lads?"

"But..."

"But what!" scowled Harry, as he turned to face Darren, a young lad who had only just come into the bar.

"Well", Darren said timidly "I was coming home from work last night about half five, and as I passed the station I saw Stanley on the platform, just as the train was pulling in."

"So what?" said Harry, by now getting impatient. He wanted to hear what the lad had to say, but there were other customers to serve. Jim and the other regulars turned round just in time to catch the lad's reply.

"Well, I swear to God, I saw him get on it!"

# OLD HAUNTS

"See that!"

"What?" came the bemused reply.

"That over there!" said Jason in exasperation.

"You're losing it" replied Daryl, shaking his head in disbelief.

"No, I'm sure I saw someone moving across the front of the shed. You know, like I saw the other night".

A look from Daryl told Jason all that he needed to know - Daryl thought he was going mad. Maybe he was, for ever since he'd started work at Botanic Gardens depot, he'd noticed a shadowy figure darting around the entrance to the shed at the stabling point.

Daryl chipped in "Just get on with checking the coolant levels on this 158 unit, and let the ghosts take care of themselves". With that he chuckled to himself, and wandered off down the ballast to see if there was any repair work noted in the driver's log book.

"I know what I saw" muttered Jason to himself, as he walked down the other side of the multiple unit.

Strolling away from the railway workers, and towards Hymers College, I thought "They must be blind!" and then laughed out loud, or as loud as a ghost can.

"Loud enough to wake the dead!" brought another fit of giggles on as I slipped through the security fence, over the school grounds, and towards Spring Bank, clutching my well worn summer 1957 edition of abc British Railway Locomotives Part 4, Eastern, N.E. and Scottish

Regions.

I better introduce myself. My name is Steven, and I've been dead since 1958. It will probably seem like a long time to you, but time's something I've plenty of. Botanic Gardens engine shed was an old haunt of mine, along with Dairycoates, but this depot was always my favourite. The shed gave me some great moments, as well as my final ones.

By now you'll be thinking 'If you're dead, then how come you're still walking around railway premises in the middle of the night?'

That's a good question, and one I'll try to answer, although it doesn't always make sense to me, which is hardly surprising, since according to the facts, I have no senses at all, being dead.

Like a lot of kids during the fifties, I was mad about trains, and at any and every opportunity I'd rush off to visit one, or all of the Hull depots. Diesel multiple units had taken over the Withernsea and Hornsea trains in January 1957, but in the late fifties, there was still a great deal of steam activity around Hull. Dairycoates was the biggest depot, handling mostly freight traffic, and was some distance away from my home off Spring Bank. Springhead wasn't so far, but the writing was on the wall for the former Hull and Barnsley Railway line, and it closed to through traffic in late 1958, which, incidentally was after my time. Botanic Gardens' allocation of locomotives was mostly for passenger work, and as such, it saw some of the glamour engines that visited Hull. My favourite locos were the D49 4-4-0s, which had just started to be withdrawn in 1957. It was also my nearest engine shed, and I would skulk in any time that I had half an hour to spare. All these trips were highly illegal of course, and if the foreman saw me, I was off like a shot towards the cover of the allotments or Hymers College. I'd hide in the bushes until he was called away to more pressing business, and then continue my stealth attack on the numbers of the engines on shed. But it wasn't just me that could be stealthy, and one night, with all my concentration focussed on a rampaging railway employee, a bigger and more deadly predator stole up on me, in the form of a local B1 4-6-0. People say things like 'He won't have felt a thing' or 'It would have been mercifully quick', but it didn't seem at all like that to me! The engine alone weighed over seventy one tons, and the tender added another fifty two to the tally. That's how my life came to be extinguished one misty winter night in January 1958. When you're hit by that, you don't come back. Again, that's what folk say, but I have come back, time and time again.

After the initial shock, it took some time to get used to being dead, but at least I didn't have to go to school, or be in at a certain hour! However, I did expect to find either oblivion, or preferably, rest in Heaven. I found neither. It's said that if a soul dies a sudden and violent death, they can never rest. Now, I don't know if that's true, but I seem doomed eternally to visit Botanic Gardens depot, even though I'm dead, steam has been dead nearly as long, and the depot is now only a pale shadow of its former self.

I've seen them all come and go. The D49s, J72 tanks, V3s, K3 2-6-0s, and even at last those Hull stalwarts, the B1s. I'd give anything to see a WD 2-8-0 now. How they used to clank slowly over Botanic Gardens level crossing in the days when the station was still open, and trundle down to a stand at the signals at Victoria Crossing. The Paxman 0-6-0 diesels sent to replace them didn't last long, neither did the Clayton Bo-Bos that followed. Soon after, the line past the depot was removed. The Trans-Pennine diesel multiple units then followed all this sad entourage on that final journey to the breaker's yard, leaving Botanic Gardens as a stabling point on a truncated spur for visiting units, and a very occasional locomotive. How are the mighty fallen!

To while away the time, I took to visiting the railwaymen in the twilight hours, or if I got really bored, I'd go and visit my grave in Chanterlands Avenue Cemetery, and throw the flowers all over. It's nice to think that people still remember me, but what use are flowers to a train spotter? Taunting the men at the depot seemed more like fun at first, but now I've grown weary of the game, and no one notices anyway, or that's how it seemed until last month. Then they took on a new fitter's assistant, I've heard other workers call him Jason. I don't know how, or why, but he does seem to notice me as I wander around the remains of the old shed, looking for that one last cop, when the days for copping that one last engine are surely long gone. I'd like to rest in peace now. Maybe someday I'll get to that great shed bash in the sky, and spend all day eating cucumber sandwiches, and watching the giants of steam storm past in scenes reminiscent of their glory days.

"How's the job going?" came a cry from the kitchen.

"Fine, mum" was Jason's unconvincing reply as he walked into the room, and dropped his rucksack next to the table.

Looking up from the sink, she continued "You don't sound too sure. You've got to give it a chance, you've only been there a month. Things will settle down, you'll see".

Jason slumped into his favourite chair, and as he took off his work boots, he asked "Is there a cup of tea on the go?"

"I'll put the kettle on now, son". With that, she filled the kettle and flicked the switch to turn it on. "There's something wrong, I can tell. I haven't been your mother for twenty-two years without becoming a bit of a mind reader. Come on, tell me what it is".

Realising that his mother was not going to budge, Jason thought for a moment before saying hesitantly "It's not the job as such, the other guys are fine, and the place is O.K.". He then paused and rubbed his chin, before continuing "I keep seeing this shape, or figure, when I'm on the night shift".

"What sort of shape?" asked his mum inquisitively. With that, the kettle boiled, giving both parties chance to gather their thoughts. She mashed the tea, glanced over her shoulder and said "Go on".

Jason lent over the side of the chair, picked up his trainers and replied "Well, it's only vague, sort of out of the corner of my eye, but it looks like a kid darting around the tracks". He then put his trainers on before adding "But it's only hazy and I could be mistaken. It's just me, none of the other blokes seem to see it. Maybe I'm just tired and adjusting to shift work. I'll just have to get used to it, railway work is all about shifts".

With that, he put his shoes on. His mother poured the tea and handing Jason his cup, she commented "Well, it's a good job, so don't you go causing trouble in your first month".

Just then, Jason's grandmother, Betty, walked into the kitchen, and seeing the freshly made pot of tea said cheerily "Is there one in the pot for me, Julie? Hi, Jason, I hope that you're looking after your mum".

"Always do" came her grandson's reply.

"But he's just been getting me worried about his job, telling me about something going on at work. Apparently, he's been seeing things. Something like the ghost of a child when he's on night shift. He says he's the only one that sees it. They'll be thinking he's crackers if he keeps that up".

No one could have predicted the old lady's response. With a crash, the cup of tea that she'd been drinking fell to the floor, and shattered on the tiles.

Her daughter rushed over to her side "What on earth is up, mam? You've gone white as a sheet. Come on, sit down. Jason, get out of that chair and give your grandma a hand".

Mother and son eased Betty into the chair.

Worried, Julie asked "You alright, Mam? What was that all about, for heaven's sake?"

Betty, visibly shaken, then proceeded to tell the following story, which was to have an impact on all in the room.

"You work at Botanic Gardens engine shed, don't you, Jason?"

The young man nodded to agree, somewhat puzzled.

"I used to have a brother, Steven. He died a long time ago, even before your mam was born. He was railway mad, forever hanging around the station, or the crossings, or anywhere there were steam engines. His favourite spot was the engine shed at Botanic Gardens. He'd sneak in there any time he had the chance and collect engine numbers. That was his downfall".

"What do you mean, grandma?"

The air was electric when the reply came "He was run over there by an engine one night in 1958!"

Taken aback, Julie blurted out "You never told me that before, Mam, and anyhow, what's that got to do with Jason?"

"I know I probably should have told you, but" hesitating, she cried "I thought it might upset you!"

Julie handed her a hanky "There, there, go on cry".

When Betty had stopped sobbing, she added "I always visit his grave once a month, and put my favourite flowers, pink carnations on it, but when I visit the next time I keep finding that someone has thrown them all over the place".

"Probably vandals" Jason chipped in.

Betty's response came quickly. "Then why were no other graves disturbed? No, I took it to mean something, and so I visited a spiritualist. I know you're not supposed to, but I wanted some sort of explanation. He told me that Steven's soul was probably unhappy, sort of in limbo, in need of rest. I asked him how I could help, and he didn't seem to have any answers, so I let the matter drop".

"But what has this to do with Jason starting his job as a fitter's assistant?"

Staring hard at her grandson, Betty remarked "You're the first in the family to work on the railway, aren't you?"

Jason muttered "Aye, I am".

"And you're the only one to see this ghost".

The room fell silent, then Betty continued "I can't explain it, but it just might be that you're seeing your great uncle".

Now Jason had never been what you might call spiritual, but somehow his grandma's story had hit him hard in a spot that he hadn't realised existed.

"So you think that because we're kind of related".

"But you are most definitely related!" Betty interrupted.

"Yeah, O.K., because we're related, then I somehow sort of see him. Is that what you're saying?"

"I think so, Jason. Maybe it's fate that you should get a job there. Perhaps you're the one to help him find rest, who knows?" A gentle smile crossed his grandmother's face. "I better be off now. We'll talk about this later."

Betty got up and opened the back door, "Bye, Julie. Bye, Jason" and walked down the garden path.

70

Such a thought would never have crossed the lad's mind, but over the coming days, that germ of an idea took hold and grew. Could it be possible that he could help his great uncle find rest?

Jason could apply himself when he had to, and so he pondered who might be able to help with this particular dilemma. His grand mother had obviously not been too happy to visit a spiritualist, and he hadn't been able to offer much joy. "I'll try our local vicar" he thought.
So it was that one day when he was off work, he found himself knocking on the door of the vicarage.
"Can I help?" came a voice from behind a beard and a pair of spectacles, as the door swung open.
"I've come for some help about a relative" came the tentative reply.
"Then come in, I'm just preparing Sunday's sermon, but that can wait for a short while. Would you like a cup of tea?"
Stepping through the door and down the corridor, Jason answered "Thanks, that would be nice".
Jason was shown into a large study room, and a few minutes later, the vicar returned with suitable refreshment.
After offering the young man his cup of tea, the vicar sat down and started the conversation with "Now, before we go any further, let me introduce myself, I'm Brian, and you are....?"
"I'm Jason. Jason Whitaker".
"Good, in what way can I be of service to this relative of yours?"

Not one to beat about the bush, Jason came straight out with "My grandma says that I've a great uncle who died in a railway accident in 1958, and still can't find rest". Realising how confused this statement sounded, Jason then promptly shut up, and looked down into his drink. Now as luck, or fate, would have it, Jason had come to just the right man, for the vicar was a former railwayman and enthusiast, although out of touch with the current railway scene. Furthermore, he had been personally involved in several exorcisms, including one with a particularly nasty poltergeist.

"When and where did your relative die?" Brian asked as sensitively as he could.

"Botanic Gardens engine shed in January 1958. His name was Steven Ward, and he was hit by a steam engine while he was trainspotting on the shed".

Brian gently sank back into his chair and mulled over this new information. Then it was though a light had switched on in his brain, and he went across to the extensive bookshelves. Hovering around a certain section, he pulled out an old note book, and fumbling through the faded pages, pronounced "I think what I'm looking for will be here. This is the church record book from 1958".

Brian soon came to the entries for the required date and continued "Yes, buried January 22$^{nd}$ in Chanterlands Avenue Cemetery, aged thirteen. Service by Reverend Drury. Tragic, yes tragic".

Putting the book down, this experienced man of the cloth cheered Jason up with "I think that I just might be able to help. However, I'm not promising anything".

With this, Jason put down his cup, and looked up.

"It seems that sometimes, if someone suffers a violent death, their soul can't find peace, and they keep revisiting the scene of their demise, in this case, Botanic Gardens railway depot. I know this may sound strange, but have you, or any of your relatives been aware of his presence since his death?"

Jason then informed Brian of what his grandma had said, and of his own personal experiences when on the night shift.

"That sounds true to my own experience in these matters. The disturbed grave and the shadowy appearances at the shed would also tally with the stories that I've read. Now we have to find a way to assist Steven find the peace that I'm sure that he is looking for. That's the difficult part. Can you leave this with me for a few days? I'll contact colleagues who are more knowledgeable in these matters than me, and get back to you as soon as I can".

With that, Jason thanked the vicar, and leaving the vicarage, he walked down the street with a lighter heart, having taken some action, albeit only minor. His heart might not have been so light, if he'd known the mountain that he would soon have to climb.

True to his word, Brian rang Jason a week later, asking him to drop in at the vicarage as soon as he could.

Finding himself in the study once more, Jason asked anxiously "Is there any hope then?"

As they both sat down, Brian said authoritatively "Well, I do have something to report. Firstly, it seems that a simple exorcism is unlikely to work, but we could try if you want. The general consensus was, that what seems more likely to succeed is for the lost soul to confront the incident that led to his demise".

Undiplomatically, Jason piped up "What does that mean in English?"

Brian's heart went out to the lad, for he knew what he was really saying. "If Steven could see the engine that killed him, it could bring what we call closure, that is, an acceptance of what had happened to him. He should rest in peace then".

Jason was crestfallen. How could Steven, a dead boy, meet up with a steam engine? Steam engines on the national network had vanished long before he was born. In fact, probably about the time his mam was at junior school. Sure, there were engines on heritage lines, puffing up and down a few miles of preserved track, but what were the odds of the actual locomotive that killed Steven still being around, nearly fifty years after he'd died. Nil, that's what the odds were.

"Thanks for your help, vicar, but I don't see how that helps me. The steam engine that struck him will have been scrapped long ago".

There are times in life when the toast falls butter side down, but just occasionally, the reverse is true.

"Not so fast, Jason, I think you're getting a little help from above, because I contacted friends who are really clued up on the railway scene, and one of them assured me that the engine involved in the fatality was B1 61306".

"So what!" was Jason's dismissive reply.

The vicar's face positively beamed as he replied "Luckily for you, B1 61306 is preserved. It's still around, in service!"

This fresh piece of information felled Jason. Collapsing into the chair, he exclaimed "Thank God!"

"Not so fast. To borrow a phrase from another religion, if Mohammed can't come to the mountain, the mountain will have to come to Mohammed. Put simply, Steven, being dead, cannot visit the railway location where 61306 is preserved. Therefore, for the plan to succeed, the engine will have to come to him. That's no simple matter these days".

How right he was, thought Jason. He'd only been in the job a few weeks, but he'd heard stories of track access charges, privatisation, fragmentation, penalty clauses, the blame culture and loads of other things that seemed too heavy for him. He could already picture the faces of people in authority when he asked for a steam locomotive to visit Hull, just on the whim that this might, and it was a big might, help a dead relative to rest in his grave. Fat chance, give up right now, Jason lad.

He thanked the vicar for his efforts, and left the vicarage with a heavy heart. By the time that he had trudged home, he'd decided to drop the matter. Get your head down, concentrate on the job, don't do anything daft, they think you're that already. These thoughts went through his mind as he slumped into bed that night, and that's how the matter would have stood, but for an incident at the depot soon afterwards.

"I'll just be a minute, I need another lamp, this one's playing up" Daryl's words sounded down the corridor, as Jason walked out of the warm office and into the rain that had been driving in hard from the east all day. It was just after midnight on a cold January night, and a 156 unit had come on shed for an 'A' exam. With his head down, and hood up, he trudged across the concrete to where the multiple unit stood, clicking to itself as the engine cooled down.

"Oh no!" Steven cried. He had ghosted onto the shed a minute or two earlier. No east wind, or biting cold could afflict him these days, but what he saw as he passed the shed entrance sent a chill through his astral frame. He'd seen Jason wander out of the door, and with his face screened, walk towards the tracks. What he also saw, but Jason did not seem to be aware of, was another diesel multiple unit drifting down from the running lines at Argyll Street, and onto the shed.
"What can I do?" thought Steven. He knew that Jason was somehow aware of him, but whether that could save him in this situation was open to question. What could a ghost do, but try to frighten the life out of the very person who was in danger of losing theirs.

Jason stepped over the first track that he came to, mumbling to himself "Even Steven's ghost wouldn't be out on a night like this". With that, an icy blast of freezing air threw him back. He fell to the floor, and looking up from the unforgiving ballast, his heart leapt. There, not three feet away, was the diesel multiple unit which, with deadly accuracy, had been bearing down on him. From this position of safety, but not comfort, Jason just managed to catch a momentary glimpse of Steven's ghost, before the passing train separated them both. When the unit had passed, all was still and dark once more.

"What you doing on the deck?" Daryl, with lamp in hand had arrived. "Come on, we've got work to do!"

There was no immediate response from Jason, and so Daryl realised that there was something amiss. Now Daryl wasn't a soft touch, but he knew that the lad hadn't been himself lately. "Seen the ghost again?"

"I think so" came Jason's tentative reply "Just now".

Offering Jason a hand, he helped him to his feet and said "You O.K. to help us with the 158 job?"

"Yeah, I think so".

The two men carried out their duties on the resident multiple units, and an hour later, in the comfort of the mess room, Jason blurted out the whole story.

To his surprise, Daryl seemed more understanding than previously. "I could see that you were shook up, and I know I haven't seen this ghost. In fact, I've never seen a ghost, an' I don't believe in them, but when you work with someone, you're a team, an' you look after each other, get me?"

Jason nodded his agreement "Thanks". Pausing, he had another swig of tea, before adding "I didn't believe in ghosts 'till I started here, but I do know what I saw, and it definitely ain't part of this world."

When Jason got out of bed the following afternoon, he

marched downstairs and said resolutely to his mam "I'm gonna do it".

"Do what, son?"

"I'm gonna try and get that engine on shed for Steven's sake".

Looking up from her magazine, Julie questioned "Why the change of heart? You said it would be too much trouble."

With that, the door opened and Betty walked in "Hi there, I've brought you some biscuits".

"Hi, Mam, thanks for those. Jason's just told me he's going to do summat about what the vicar told him a while ago."

Betty sat down next to Jason "That's good, I was hoping you'd do it, but this is rather sudden."

The bombshell fell "Steven saved my life last night".

"I told you that fate had something to do with it!" said Betty triumphantly. "Tell us what happened then".

Jason recounted the story before adding "I can't let it rest now. I'm sure that the blast of icy white mist that raced past me was his ghost. If it hadn't made me jump out of my skin, I could have been joining Steven in the grave today. I owe it to him, an' everyone else, to get this sorted".

His mind was obviously set. Betty thanked him profusely, and his mother made them all a cup of coffee. So life went on.

Brian, the vicar, through his contacts, was able to get the owner's details for 61306. Jason, never much of a letter writer, now had a crash course in the art. Yes, the loco was active, but no tours near Hull were planned, and unfortunately the boiler certificate was due to expire in March the following year. "Over twelve months, plenty of time", thought Jason.

How wrong he was! Further enquiries brought home to Jason the mountain that he had to climb in order to bring one to Mohammed, or in this case, to Steven's ghost at Botanic Gardens. Network Rail heaped problem upon problem, route availability, fire risks, gauging concerns, the list went on and on. But Jason was not deterred. With the Brian's help, he contacted tour operators, and together they presented their plans to them. Still no joy, and that's how it would have stayed, with the months ticking away, but for a fortunate coincidence.

All Jason and Brian's correspondence had been aimed at the managerial level of Network Rail, but as luck would have it, one letter ended up on a director's desk. Angus Macpherson was a no nonsense sort of individual, who'd done very well for himself, rising from humble beginnings to become the epitome of a self made man. However, he'd lost a son in a railway accident, which had left a mark on his otherwise impenetrable exterior. Without Jason and Brian knowing it, their tale had touched him, and he started to pull strings, but on one point he would not budge. On no account was the locomotive to enter Botanic Gardens stabling point. It could use the West Parade North Junction to Anlaby Road Junction avoiding line, but that was to be the limit of its visit to Hull. It was to be a passing guest, skirting gently around KC Stadium, with the engine drifting tantalisingly close to the depot that was its old haunt.

So it was that a railtour from London to York and Scarborough, returning via Goole to Doncaster was organised for February. 61306 was to haul the special on the Yorkshire leg of the tour, from York to Doncaster via Scarborough and Hull. With just two weeks left before the B1's boiler certificate expired, it was cutting things fine, but in the light of current railway operation, it was nothing short of a miracle, as Brian said when Jason informed him of the arrangements.

"But not miracle enough" exclaimed Brian to Jason, as they discussed the coming events in the vicar's study that frosty January morning.

Brian continued "61306 has to visit Botanic Gardens shed to help. In fact, it has to be on shed when Steven makes one of his sporadic visits. It was always a long shot, but we've had uncanny luck so far. I'm sure the Lord must be helping, for there is no other way that I can account for the progress that we've made. I've told you before, Jason, God sometimes uses human hands to do his work. We'll have to hope that he's still working on someone's heart somewhere on this one. Keep believing!" With these positive words, he cheered up Jason as he left.

Daryl was a team player, and just as he felt that he had to help Jason, he could understand that the lad felt duty bound to help a relative, albeit one long dead. He'd been on the railway for over ten years, and so had learnt a trick or two. As the date of the tour approached he got hold of details of the trip from a signalman that he knew. Plain as day, there were the timings, Cottingham 18.42, Hessle Road Junction 19.06. The footnotes added ominously, 'Under no circumstances is the steam locomotive to be watered in Hull, or in the event of failure, to be stabled in Hull'.

"No visit to Botanic there then" mumbled Daryl to no one in particular. Reluctantly, he told Jason the news. He could see that his mate was crest fallen, but he knew that Jason had done all that was humanly possible to get man (or ghost) and machine to meet.

Jason was on the night shift on the fateful day in February. He couldn't bear to watch the locomotive pass so near, and yet so far, from his intended location, and so he spent the day out at Withernsea. He got home, changed his clothes and trudged down to the depot at his appointed clocking on time. With great reluctance he walked down Kimberley Street and through the depot entrance, knowing that all his endeavours had come to nought. It had taken him over a year to get this far, and with the engine's boiler certificate due to expire within days, it would be a long time, indeed if ever, before the B1 came to Hull again. With these thoughts clouding his mind, he ambled past the site of the redundant turntable, a relic from the days of steam, and into the shed yard, where he was greeted by the biggest surprise of his short life. There, larger than life, was 61306 tucked down the stores road. Jason stumbled, letting out the exclamation "What the hell!"

"It's there alright!" Daryl called, leaning out of the office door "Want to know what happened?"

Jason rushed towards the fitter "Sure, you bet!"

Smiling, Daryl explained "It passed Beverley on time, but just after Cottingham, the fireman suspected that they had a hot box. Sure enough, as it passed KC Stadium and got onto Anlaby Road Junction, the wheels locked up solid. They couldn't move it forward or aft. The inspector on board demanded that the loco be detached and stabled until the damage could be assessed. It seems that despite what the notice had said, nothing that Network Rail could do or say would change his mind. He wasn't budging any more than the engine was! Anyway, they had to clear the tracks for normal services, so they managed to get hold of a class 66 from the docks, and after the offending bearing had cooled down a little, the diesel dragged the steamer in here. The 66 then took the special forward to Doncaster, over two hours late".

Jason was overwhelmed by the events that Daryl had recounted, but coming to his senses, he brushed past him, saying "I better clock on".

While Daryl was on the phone, Jason wandered down the yard to the locomotive. The yard was lit, but the stores road was always the shady end of the shed. Only the glint of its clean smokebox door caught the eye. As he approached the stricken locomotive, the clouds parted and the moon shone out. In the silver light, he could make out a smoky shape drifting from the direction of Hymers College and towards the buffer beam of 61306. It was Steven!

Jason froze to the spot. Should he keep away, or should

he rush to greet the ghost that had caused him so much hard work, and to be perfectly honest, pain? Mixed emotions tore him apart, and so he watched, mesmerised, as the outline of the figure reached the engine. Then something awesome happened. The ghost touched the buffer beam of 61306, and seemed to flesh out and take form. There, not ten yards in front of Jason, stood a boy in grey trousers and a duffle coat.

Jason half managed to lift his arm in welcome, but it was as though his body wouldn't react. He tried to call, but only strangled sounds passed his lips. The boy seemed to run his hand tenderly along the cold steel of the engine's frame, and then he turned his gaze upon Jason, who was frozen in the moment. Was it a trick of the light, or was that a smile on the boy's face?

Jason was not to know, for the clouds scudded across the winter sky, and in the watery light, Steven's shape lost its definition, and dissolved away into the night air.

"Come on, Jason!" Daryl's call broke the spell, and Jason turned to see his mate striding towards him.

"I thought I'd find you down here, seen your ghost yet?" Jason nodded and pointed "Over there, in front of the buffer beam." He then looked down at the floor before adding "I don't think he'll be back. I think 61306 has done the trick."

Sympathetically, Daryl murmured "I hope so. I hope so. Come on, we've work to do." With that, the fitter and assistant walked towards the cab of a soulless 158 D.M.U..

It seemed like a long shift that night, but Jason rang home just before he left next morning to tell his mum what had gone on that night. Therefore, it was no big surprise that when Jason got home, he found the living room full of people. Of course there was his mother, and it was of little surprise that Betty was also there.

More of a surprise was the sight of Brian, amply filling the easy chair with his sturdy frame. Seeing Jason's puzzled expression, he explained "Your mother called me first thing, and so I came straight round."

"Hello, son, you O.K.?" A mother's concern as always "I'll make a pot of tea."

Betty spoke next "Did you see him? You know, Steven".

Jason, tired after his shift, slumped into his favourite chair "Yes, I saw him, grandma. I think he can rest now."

Brian chipped in "Let's hope so. There is never any guarantee in this kind of affair. We're dealing with forces that we can't possibly imagine, but Jason has done all he could, and he's to be commended for that."

"But how can we be sure that Steven will rest in peace now?" Julie's question was interrupted by a knock at the front door, so she answered it, and in walked Daryl.

"Hello everyone, I hope I'm not disturbing anything" was the fitter's slightly awkward welcome.

"Do you want a cup of tea?" said Julie reaching for the teapot.

"No, I'll not be staying. Got to get to bed you know. I only called because of Jason's problem with the depot ghost". Realising the clumsiness of this comment, he chuckled nervously and added "After Jason had gone off shift, I went down to the steam loco before anyone came to repair it and take it away. I found these on the buffer beam."

The light of the early morning sun fell upon the items in Daryl's hand, a pink carnation and a very battered abc trainspotting book. It fell open at the title page, dated summer 1957.

The vicar, sensing the enormity of the event, spoke quietly and reverently "It is finished". There followed a long silence, when the noise of the world outside; the traffic, the footsteps, the shouts, drifted into the living room, but were no part of the thoughts of those gathered there.

Jason broke the silence "I know that I did all I could, but I didn't make an engine break down to order. I still can't believe it's really happened".

"No, of course you didn't make an engine break down, Jason, but there are more things in heaven and earth". It was Betty's voice, as she turned to face Brian "I'm sure the vicar will agree."

"Of course. I told Jason that I believed we'd had a little divine intervention in Steven's case."

Agitated, Jason got up from his chair "That's fine as it goes, Brian, but the Network Rail notice specifically stated that the loco was not, under any circumstances, to be stabled in Hull. Get round that one, if you can!"

The vicar smiled "We all prayed for a miracle." At this point everyone muttered agreement, particularly Betty. Brian continued "I've told you before, Jason, God sometimes uses human hands to do his work. In this case, those hands belonged to an old railway colleague of mine. The inspector on board the fateful train was an old friend. Of course, only God could foresee that 61306 would develop an overheated main bearing, but only an accredited railway inspector could over-ride the Network Rail order!"

Betty exclaimed "Well, all in all, it's been one miracle after another!"

Opening the door to leave, Daryl added "An' here's another one. Before Jason came to Botanic Gardens, I didn't believe in ghosts, but after seeing what's gone on here, I swear on the Bible, I reckon there must be sommat in it!"

With these words, he said goodbye to everyone and Julie let him out of the front door.

Did Steven find peace at last? Well, I'll let the reader be the judge of that.

Jason did well in his job and Daryl and he became great mates. Did Jason see Steven's ghost again? No, never, not on starlit nights when the frost was so keen that the air would stop the breath of any mortal. Nor in the dark hours when the fogs of November would swirl absentmindedly around Jason as he performed his duties at the forlorn depot, and definitely not after midnight when the hard rains driven by the east wind stripped flesh from bone.

Betty and Julie took turns to look after Steven's grave. The pink carnations, undisturbed, looked glorious in the first warmth of the spring sunshine.

# POINTS OF NO RETURN

"There is nothing for it, I'll have to stay late", thought Simon. It had been a busy day, with meeting after meeting, and numerous phone calls to be made, and he still had a report to finish. He would have loved to return home on his regular, the 18.10 from Liverpool Street, but a finish three hours beyond that looked more likely. That was the sacrifice that you had to make if you wanted to get to the top, for Simon Barclay was an ambitious man.

Politics and government are like magnets that attract people with ambitions of wielding power, and Simon was such a man. He'd entered local politics in the early 1960s, and with his charm, intelligence and utter ruthlessness, he'd soon come to the attention of the movers and shakers of the time. By 1965 he was an M.P., and before the decade was out, he was an important member of the party's transport policy committee. He'd made unpopular decisions, but they had done his career no harm whatsoever. He could see which way the wind was blowing, and road transport was in, and the railways definitely out. He always blew with the prevailing wind, and was never slow to seize the main chance with both hands. In so doing, he'd amassed a personal fortune along the way, not dishonestly of course, but he had made a few enemies. Not that they dared to oppose him, for no man who crossed him prospered for long. If there were any points in the past where his conscience had troubled him, his aspirations soon stifled these qualms and so his career continued on its relentless rise. There were mutterings and rumours, but Simon was a powerful man, and few dared to voice their concerns other than in the corners of the wine bars and cafes that have sprung up around the political establishments, like parasites feeding on the crumbs that fall from the master's table.

The rain spattered on the window of his office as he busied himself with the final draft of his report on rail privatisation. He glanced up from his computer as the clock dolourously chimed out eight, and then at the pitch black world outside.
"I should do well out of this" Simon muttered to himself, and then his fingers returned to feverishly rattling over the keyboard once more.
The fragmentation of the railways offered a man of Simon's undoubted skills enormous potential for gain, for there were so many small companies to be spun off, so many share options, and so many non-executive directorships to be garnered. Not only that, but his colleagues and political superiors thought that the proposals he'd outlined were sure to see his promotion to the highest ranks, and maybe be a vote winner too. For him, it was the perfect policy combination. Even at this late hour, his cronies would still ring up, and it was after nine when he finished the document and rose from the chair. Stretching himself, he then pulled a pocket timetable out of his attache case, and fingered his way through the slim document to find the service he needed.

"Damn, I've just missed one!" he cursed as he reached for his overcoat.

He strode out of his office into the blast of the December storm, and had no problem hailing a cab. Soon he was walking briskly into Liverpool Street Station. Glancing at the destination board, and then his watch, he realised that he had time for a quick coffee. His departure, the 22.15, was the last train of the day, and was timetabled to scoop up the last of London's overworked commuters, and the few people who chose to visit that part of Essex late at night for pleasure. The mumbled words over the station P.A. system spoke of a slight delay due to a points failure near Stratford. This may have been correct, but Simon secretly suspected that it was more likely to be some poor attempt to disguise the inefficiency of nationalised railways. What Simon didn't hear, as he made small talk while placing his order, was that his train was subject to a platform change, from 9 to 6. Having drunk his coffee, he strode down platform 9 at 22.10, blissfully unaware that the carriages before him would not be taking him to his home station that night. No sooner had he closed the carriage door than the train was away. How prompt, he thought, rather more efficient than the system has been of late. If there had been a points failure, it certainly hadn't affected his departure. In fact, according to his watch, the train had left three minutes early. Not that Simon minded of course, for the sooner he was away, then the sooner he'd be home.

The train was poorly patronised, and as it clattered over

the pointwork at the platform end, Simon took off his overcoat and looked around to see that he was the only occupant of the carriage. That's good, he thought to himself, for he wanted to catch up on more paperwork on the way home, and not to be distracted by idle chatter or one half of an inane mobile phone conversation. The rain was still lashing down, and only the occasional lights of a passing station caused Simon to look up from his duties. The train rumbled on into the night, and just after 23.00 the carriage lurched.

"What the hell!" Simon cried, as his papers spilled from his lap and fell to the floor. He gathered them up, put them on the seat and then peered through the window. He didn't recognise the location, and he had certainly never noticed poor trackwork near there before. He then sat down and recalled the last station that he had noticed and realised he wasn't far from home.

"We're somewhere near the junction to Binchley then, or where it used to be" he uttered to no one.

The train rattled on, unperturbed by his deliberations, and eventually slowed down as it entered a rural station. Home, thought Simon, but as he stepped out onto the platform edge and shut the door behind him, it looked nowhere like his prosperous Essex village. The rain had stopped, and in the damp night air, he could make out a brick station building, with a welcoming glow from a blazing fire in the waiting room opposite him.

"How quaint!" He said to himself "But it's not my stop!" The station appeared to be more like one of the charming little halts that you see on preserved railways, manicured for the tourist and suitably packaged for the maximum nostalgic effect, even down to the gas lighting.

"The train must have been diverted onto some heritage line, but it's a ghastly mistake all the same!" Simon blurted out.

"It's no mistake" came a disembodied voice from the platform end.

Simon could dimly make out a tall figure drawing nearer to him through the mist.

At that moment, the train jolted, and then it was heading into the winter night in the direction from which it had come. With a final swirl of mist, the rear buffer beam, and then the red tail lights were swallowed up in the all consuming blackness.

"Tickets please" continued the authoritative voice, as the steps crunched ever nearer on the gravel.

Instinctively, Simon reached for his wallet, before pausing and saying "But no one collects tickets now, all the checking is done on the train."

The man, now visible as a smartly dressed railway official, had reached Simon, and seemed undeterred by this reply, "Tickets please, sir."

Reluctantly, Simon drew his ticket from his wallet, and handed it to him.

There was a slight pause before the official commented "I'm afraid this ticket isn't valid here, sir."

"What do you mean?" asked Simon, then hesitating for a second, he continued truculently "And where the hell is here anyway?"

"Binchley, sir."

For once in his life, Simon was lost for words. "Binchley, how could it be Binchley?", Simon pondered to himself. When he had recovered his poise, he decided to take command of the situation and launched in with "Don't be ridiculous, this can't be Binchley. Now be a good chap and stop playing games with me. Do you realise who I am?"

Without hesitation, the railwayman replied "Mr Simon Barclay".

Simon stumbled backwards, and came to rest on a wooden bench placed there thoughtfully for weary travellers. After gathering his wits, he carefully placed his valuable attache case next to him, whereupon he noticed the word 'Binchley' clearly embossed on the back of the seat.

Seeing Simon's discomfort, the official continued "Yes, this is Binchley Station, you are Mr Simon Barclay, and I am Walter Fairclough."

Now somewhat humbled, the politician uttered "I don't recognise that name, I don't believe that I've ever seen you before in my life."

Standing near one of the station's gaslights, Walter replied "No, you've never met me, and I most certainly have never met you. That didn't stop you closing my station back in 1968."

For a man who was used to wielding power, Simon's rebuff "What do you mean 'my' station?" was decidedly weak.

"I was the station master at Binchley, and as it turned out, the last station master here, for I was working here when you had the line closed" was Walter's response.

It's all some sort of joke thought Simon, but I'll humour the man anyway, for it is late, and I need to get home. "I didn't close the line, you must be mistaken, Mr Fairclough."

Walter's reply was immediate and damning "I am not wrong, Mr Barclay. I know all about you. No doubt you can talk your way out of most sticky situations, but not this time, for I know the facts."

Having composed himself once more, Simon said, almost nonchalantly "What facts?"

"That as a young M.P., you were on the transport sub-committee in 1966 that sealed this line's fate. You had the casting vote, which could have swung the decision either way. You chose to deal the death blow, and for why? Because that vote suited your political masters and helped you up the greasy pole. You gained your promotion, and we all lost our livelihoods. The railway was the heart of the town. One by one, the shops closed, people drifted away to more prosperous places, and the place slowly died."

Crestfallen, the man who had risen so far could not believe what he had just heard and yelled out "How the hell could you know about that meeting? It was behind closed doors, and anyway that was years ago."

"I know" was the cryptic reply

Fumbling for his mobile phone, Simon blurted out "I'm fed up with this senseless game, so good night!" With that, he punched in his home number "I'll just get my wife to collect me!" However, no amount of endeavour could get any kind of signal. He was pressing all the right buttons, but to no avail.

"There must be poor reception here" he muttered.

Walter chuckled to himself and started to walk away.

After a number of attempts to bring the recalcitrant device back to life, the politician sat disconsolately down on the bench. Always the fighter, he could see only one obvious course of action, even if the humble pie stuck in his throat. He could hear Walter's steps fading away, and so he stood up and called after the railwayman politely "O.K., you've made your point. Now can you tell me how I get out of here?"

There was a long pause, before the station master's voice drifted back from a distance through the gathering gloom "You don't".

# TUNNEL VISION

"Watch out, Frank!" cried Sean, as he grabbed Frank's arm and pulled him clear of the track. Moments later, a diesel multiple unit screamed past with its horn blaring. Sean, exasperated, continued "You're getting a bit careless."

"I'm alright, my mind was elsewhere" Frank said dismissively.

"Your body will soon be following your mind elsewhere, if you don't pay a bit more attention!"

Sean had noticed for several months that Frank's heart wasn't in the job like it used to be. Frank was probably thirty years older than Sean's twenty five years, but Sean had a strong sense of self preservation, which for some reason Frank was beginning to lose.

They were both permanent way workers on the line from Leeds to Manchester via Diggle. Standedge Tunnel was part of their section, and a grim spot it could be. High on the Pennine Hills, it had the dubious distinction of having the summit of the line within its three mile length. That's a long way to walk in the dark, inspecting trackwork for faults, and undertaking routine maintenance. Frank had worked the section for many years, and some felt that he had become just a little too familiar with its stygian gloom.

Sitting down for a snack at the mouth of the tunnel, the two railwaymen chattered aimlessly around all the usual topics, TV, women, football, until Sean plucked up the courage to challenge Frank about his recent inattention. "Frank, I'm worried about you." Sean took another bite of his sandwich before adding "Mebbe I've seen too many safety videos, but you've got to keep your wits about you in this job. I know you're getting a bit fed up of it, but you're me mate, and mates look out for each other."

"You've nowt to worry about, son, I've 'ad over thirty five years experience on this job, so I could teach you a trick or two." With that, a class 66 diesel stormed past with a freight train on the up line. As the fumes drifted away in the gentle sunlight of that autumn Friday morning, Frank bit heartily into a chocolate bar before continuing triumphantly "Anyroad, I've plans, you know, to get me out of this flaming job."

This was the first time that Sean had heard of any such plans, and Frank's tone of voice suggested he was rather more dissatisfied with the job than he had guessed.

"What do you mean, plans?" Sean said quizzically.

There was a short pause as Frank gazed out over the hills, and then, looking Sean straight in the eye, he blurted out "Can you keep a secret?"

"Sure, we've been mates on the railway for seven years haven't we?"

"Bah, what's seven years! When I started walking the track, there were still steam locos working these hills. We often had to put a handkerchief over our mouths, just to be able to breathe as we stumbled through the tunnel to get to fresh air. In those days, that old tunnel bore over yonder was still in use. In fact, my first days on the railway were spent in there. They were some of the best days of my life. I'd give owt to see them again, for there was some pride in the job then. They abandoned that bore not long after I took on this length."

Frank rarely reminisced. Sean was more likely to hear diatribes about the current management, or rather, lack of it, than to hear Frank's memories of steam days. "That's as mebbe, but you asked me if I could keep a secret, an' I said yes." Sean replied with some annoyance. Frank took a swig of tea, and wiping his mouth with the back of his sleeve he said apologetically "I'm sorry, Sean, but I've 'ad enough of this job, an' I want out." He put his flask back in his bag, and continued "I've this vision of winning the lottery."
Sean laughed out loud "Yeah, an' so 'ave half the population of the country. Is that your plan? Come on Frank, you'll 'ave to do better than that."
"You may laugh, but I've a system. I've noticed certain things about the numbers, and I'm going to test my theory out."
Undeterred, Sean launched in "Don't you think that cleverer blokes than you would have noticed this by now, an' made themselves millionaires?"
Stung by these comments, Frank snapped back "Well, I do 'ave a system, but I won't be telling you! If my ideas aren't clever enough for you, then I'll try owt. I'm not stopping in this job any longer. If need be, I'll sell my soul to the Devil, if it gets me off the railway!"
Fortunately, a down express cut the conversation short, and Sean was pleased that it had. He'd never seen Frank so angry before, and as he had to work with the man for the rest of the day, he felt it best to let the matter drop.

Hardly a word passed between them as they stumbled through the bowels of the tunnel that afternoon. A great bruise of clouds had gathered by the time they left its portals again, and they trudged back to the van through driving rain. The weather put a final dampener on the day, and Sean was thankful that it was the weekend. He'll probably be O.K. by Monday morning, he thought to himself.

They were to work together at Standedge tunnel on Monday as well, and they had previously arranged to make their own way there and meet up at the tunnel entrance. It was no surprise therefore when Frank heard the crunch of ballast under foot behind him. He turned, expecting to see Sean, but was confronted by a fair young man whom he did not recognise.
"Who are you then?" was Frank's puzzled query.
Smiling, the stranger gave the cursory answer "I'm Nick."
"Where's Sean, my regular mate?" Frank said suspiciously.
"He's had an accident. I'm the temporary replacement from the agency" was the new arrival's reply.
"Damn, what happened?" Frank blurted out.
Nick's reply was noncommittal "I don't know, I was just told to report here at 08.00."
"We can't just let anyone wander around the railway, it's a dangerous place. Let me see your I.D. and paperwork." Frank was still unhappy with having a new assistant, but if all the paperwork, that is safety clearances and suchlike, were in order, he had no grounds for complaint. Time was money, and the boss

would roast him in Hell if he stopped the job without a legitimate reason. It was all down to the blame culture that prevailed on the railway now. It hadn't always been so, Frank mused to himself.

After looking over the documents, Frank reluctantly said "Well, that appears to be in order. Come wi' me. We've got to check some rail about a mile into the tunnel on the down side. There's been reports of rough riding in the area."

With that, the two men, one middle aged and disillusioned, and the other young and cocky, strode down the cess at the side of the line, and into the blackness that is Standedge Tunnel.

Frank was never seen alive again. When he didn't report back that evening, Frank's gaffer, Ken, sent another gang of track workers through the busy tunnel in search of him. There was no sign whatsoever of the experienced railwayman.

Attention then turned to Frank's mate, Sean. A visit to his flat drew a blank. At this point, Ken had the bright idea of checking the hospitals in the area. It was a long shot, but his reasoning was that if an accident had happened to either of them, then that's where they would end up.

This immediately paid dividends, for there, in the nearest hospital, was Sean. He was in a bad way though, for he had serious injuries that had put him in traction, and was still unconscious.

Ken decided to wait at the bedside to see if Sean would come round.

"You may have a long wait" said the ward nurse sympathetically.

"Then I'll wait" was Ken's robust reply "We've one worker disappeared completely, and his mate here is seriously injured. We need some answers."

With that the nurse drifted off, attending to her other duties.

It was three days before Sean opened his eyes. The search for Frank continued, checking all his usual haunts, friends, relatives, but at the time that Sean re-entered the land of the living, there was still no word of his colleague.

"Where am I?" was the predictable opening line from the young man.

"In hospital" was the equally predictable reply from Ken "You've been here since just after midnight on Sunday. You had an accident on your motorbike, don't you remember?"

"Ah, yeah" was Sean's feeble response. Then his whole expression changed, taking on the look of a frightened animal.

Ken was worried "What's wrong, Sean? You've gone as white as a ghost."

There was a murmur of agreement round the bedside of the stricken man at the last comment, but all fell silent as Sean, with some difficulty, gasped out "It weren't a ghost I saw. I don't know what the hell it was, but I hope I never see one again."

Ken thought to himself that the lad was probably delirious, but replied "What do you mean?"

There was an ominous pause before Sean explained "I was coming home from my girlfriend's house on my bike, when this thing ran in front of me."

"Thing, what thing ran in front of you?" piped up a work mate at the foot of the bed.

"A goat, or sommat like one. It was bigger than any goat I've ever seen, an' it just leapt straight at me." With that, Sean's whole body shook.

"Give him a glass of water" was Ken's practical reply.

After carefully sipping from the side of the glass, Sean continued "It looked at me with eyes that I've never seen in any animal before. They were red, blazing red. After that, I don't remember anything."

There was a knowing look around the bedside. Yes, the young lad was delirious. It was to be expected.

Matter of fact, Sean muttered "I expect Frank missed me on Monday".

A silence fell around those gathered, before Ken gathered himself together and said "Frank hasn't been seen since Monday. As far as we know, he went down to Standedge Tunnel on Monday morning, but no one's seen hide nor hair of him since."

It was Sean's turn to be dismayed "Oh no, I hope he hasn't done owt daft. He's been getting a bit careless lately, and what's more, we had an argument on Friday. The mood was like thunder when we parted at the end of the shift."

At this point, the proceedings took a spectacular turn, for a railway policeman strode up to the bed and whispered in Ken's ear. Ken's jaw dropped, and after a few moments he stood up and addressed the gathering "Frank's been found."

There were mutters of astonishment, and the word "Where?" fell from a number of lips.

"At Standedge" was Ken's sombre reply.

"But we went through the tunnel four times, an' we never saw owt!" was the comment from one of the older workers. Unabashed, Ken replied "But you didn't look in the old bore, the disused one."

"Course we didn't. He's not very likely to have an accident in there, is he?" was the crusty response.

"Well, it appears he did, for the preliminary investigation seems to suggest that he was struck by a train."

"That's impossible! There's been no locos through the old bore since steam days" blurted out the old hand.

This was all too much for Sean, who muttered "So much for his plans for the lottery" before drifting off into incoherence and then slumber.

"You keep an eye on the lad. I'm off to find out more." Ken said to two of the stalwarts at the bedside.

Ken readily identified Frank's battered body, and as Frank had no immediate family, the police asked Ken to sign for the few possessions in the dead man's pockets. Memories of steam days flooded Ken's mind as he handled Frank's clothes, for there was a distinctive tang of smoke and ash lingering over them, which made no sense to him at all. Among the coins and scribbled bits of paper was a lottery ticket for the draw the previous Saturday. "Won't do him much good now" thought Ken.

What puzzled him, as Frank's gaffer, was that such an experienced man should have started work without a lookout man. Surely Frank knew the procedures. If Sean was unable to assist Frank, which he obviously wasn't from a hospital bed, why hadn't Frank called in to get a temporary worker from the agencies? Furthermore, if Frank had been hit by a train, how did he end up in the disused bore? It was all a mystery.

When he got home, Ken rang all the agencies that supplied temporary men to their track maintenance company. None had been contacted on Monday, and therefore the agencies had supplied no one. Ken then checked the winning numbers for the lottery draw. He collapsed into his chair when he found that they were the winning numbers! He checked and re-checked, then rang up the help line available, and sure enough, this was the winning ticket. He rushed to the hospital to tell Sean, who was drinking tea through a straw when Ken arrived.

Pulling a chair to the bedside, Ken burst forth "You'll never believe what I have to tell you."

Without emotion, Sean replied "Frank had won the lottery, hadn't he."

It was Ken's turn to be overwhelmed "How the hell did you know that? I've got the ticket here, an' I've told no one else."

"Call it sixth sense" was Sean's enigmatic comment. "On Friday, he said that he'd sell his soul to the Devil for what he wanted, and what he wanted was to win the lottery and leave the railway." There was a short pause, before Sean concluded "It looks like Frank got what he wanted."

That wasn't quite the end of the tale though, for Ken was present at the preliminary enquiry the next day. The policeman who found the unfortunate man's body had observed a number of animal tracks, not dissimilar to those made by a sheep or goat, near the body. As there were no such animals in the vicinity, and even if there were, they could not possibly have inflicted such grievous wounds, this information was disregarded. The enquiry then moved on its own ponderous way, slowly sifting through the rest of the evidence.

At the end of the day, Ken, suffering from information overload and boredom, called in at the newsagents on the way home to buy some chocolate.
The owner greeted him "Hello, Ken. How's things with you? Sorry to hear about Frank, a bad do that."
"You're right there" Ken said with sadness.
The newsagent busied himself with the evening papers before he chipped in "He used to come in here every week to buy his lottery ticket, regular as clockwork. Not last Friday, though. Funny, that!"

# THE SUSPENDED SERVICE

They say that when your number's up, your number's up, but I think there are some folk, when their time is up, they don't know until someone tells 'em. Well, that's how it seemed to me, back in January 1963.

I was working at the time as a porter signalman at Hunmanby, near Filey. The station is on the Scarborough to Hull line, and somehow survived Beeching's axe. Like many lines that winter, we were having trouble keeping the trains going. The passenger trains were all diesel by then, but they had to put on a few steamers to keep things running. They were heavier, you see, an' could push through the snowdrifts better.

Anyway, I was on back shift, that is the afternoon turn, one day towards the end of the month, and arrived at the station about one. Fortunately, I lived locally and so had no problem getting to work.
"Anything running?" I said to Jack, who'd done the early turn.
"Nowt since ten" he replied "It were a steamer, an' even that 'ad trouble with a drift near Bempton. Anyway, I'm off while I can get off."
With that he trudged down the lane with his bag over his shoulder, snow circling round him as he faded into the greyness of the winter afternoon.
"They're talking of suspending the service any time!" came a disembodied voice from out of the gloom.

"Well, mebbe I'll have an easy shift then!" I shouted after him.

I had a few jobs to do at the start of the shift, mostly cleaning and dealing with lamps, but that only took a couple of hours.

"I'll get the fire in signalbox roaring" I said to no one in particular. Well that was hardly surprising as no one had been down to the station, an' no trains 'ad come in.

The snow was now settling fast, and I couldn't see anything moving that day, so I pulled out some magazines from my locker and settled down for a read. I was deep in a ghost story, when I heard the distinctive crunch of boot on hard packed snow that heralded a visitor. An icy chill brought in a stranger.

"Owt running?" said a voice laden with impending disappointment, as he closed the door behind him, almost as an afterthought.

"Not since ten" I said, raising my head slightly from the page in order to get a better view of my intruder "It's unlikely that owt will get through today."

He mumbled, "I thowt as much" to the window, as he gazed out across the tracks now lost beneath a fresh white carpet of snow.

Well here's rum company, I thought t'meself, so in order to brighten up the mood I said "I'm reading about ghosts. Don't believe in them mesen, but it passes the time."

"Naw, there's no such things as ghosts. Anyway, I've nivver seen one."

With that he paused, before continuing "Do you think there will be owt running tomorrow?"

"Mebbe, mebbe , but they're talking of suspending the service until things can get through" I replied.

His response seemed to be out of all proportion to this comment, for his whole body seemed to shudder, and after a long pause he took a deep breath and replied "Well, I better be off. I'm to meet a person at choch."

"It'll be cold down there!" I yelled after him, as he closed the door and shambled off down the platform, and soon the sound of his footsteps vanished as fast as any warmth he must have got from my fire.

"Strange meeting" I thought to myself as I glanced at the station lights. "At least it seems to have stopped snowing now."

With that I returned to my reading until it was time to go. I built up the fire for the early man next day and locked up.

"That's funny!" I said as I turned from the signalbox door.

There were no tracks where the visitor had walked. No one had been since, and no more snow had fallen.

"All a bit odd" I thought out loud.

Well, I walked home in the frozen night air, and as the cold wind off the North Sea hit me, I shivered and decided that I'd probably dreamt it all.

Yes, that was it! I'd been warm. I was reading a ghost story. I was tired, easily explained. In fact, if he'd been real, I couldn't for the life of me remember any of his features at all. He was more like a 'no-man' than a snowman!

Next day I was on back shift again, and if anything, the conditions were worse that the day before. I relieved Jack again, who confirmed that Control had suspended the service until the situation eased.

"Looks like another easy shift!" I thought, and settled down in the box for another hard afternoon's reading. Or so I thought.

I read until about seven, but then I must have fallen asleep, for I awoke with a jolt to find the fire low and a draught around my ankles. That wasn't my main concern though, for standing before me was my visitor again!

"Owt running?" came the glum voice once more.

Still dazed, I struggled for words, but must have spluttered something along the lines of "As I said was likely yesterday, they've suspended the service until further notice."

"That explains the delay" came his ambiguous response. He then headed for the door and closed it with the parting comment "Well, I better be off. I'm to meet a person at choch."

With that, he sloped off into the blackness towards the cemetery at the south end of the station, leaving me shaken. A lazy wind rolled loose snow off the Wolds and onto the drift that already seemed part of the station fittings.

I knew it wasn't a dream this time, as straight away I checked for tracks.

There were none! I wasn't dreaming it after all. At the end of my shift I went home troubled.

I said nowt to me mate the next day, as he'd probably have thought I was barmy, but as there were still no trains running, I had little else to take my mind off the matter. It was no surprise to me by then that about eight in the evening, my unwelcome guest reappeared.

The question "Owt running?" came with the same lack of interest in any likely reply from me, but I did take the trouble to look closely at him. He was well wrapped up, but I did notice that he seemed to have a very pale complexion, almost boyish, with no obvious appearance of whiskers.

The conversation passed as previously, except his final words were slightly different — "I'm to meet a person at choch. He'll be here tomorrow" being his parting shot. Well, I stoked up the fire well at the end of the shift, as next day it was my turn for early duties.

Next morning, things changed dramatically. At seven a snowplough got through, and an hour after, the 07.48 from Scarborough arrived only fifteen minutes late. The first passenger to get off was the local vicar.

"Morning, parson" I said, and on the spur of the moment added "Can you spare me a few minutes? You might be able to help me."

Thinking that he might have a new member for the flock, he smiled and said, "I've been delayed in Scarborough for three days, so I think it unlikely that a few more minutes will inconvenience me."

After dealing with the normal duties associated with the train's departure, we settled down in the signalbox to talk. This was irregular I know, but at least this visitor to the box was in the land of the living!

"What's on your mind?" the vicar kindly asked, as I mashed a pot of tea from the kettle fizzing on my stove. "Do you believe in ghosts?" I blurted as I returned the kettle to its resting place.

"Do I believe in ghosts?" he chuckled, before continuing "Well, in my line of business, it's normal to believe in life after death. Whether that would include beings that drift in and out of our sphere of existence, I don't know!" With that the whole tale poured out of me, and the minister sank back in thought in the comfy chair near the door. After I'd finished, he waited a few seconds and then said "Who do you think that your spectral visitor was?"

Perplexed, I said "I've no idea, I hoped you might know." The vicar immediately responded "Did you get a look at the fellow? He must have stood here for a while for him to have said as much as he did."

"Well, although he was obviously a man in later years, he had a very boyish, pale face" I replied.

The vicar's normal cheery disposition appeared to leave him, and was replaced by a cloud that seemed to settle on his brow.

After a long pause, the words "Perhaps, I do" fell quietly from his lips.

He continued "I've been here since 1952, but prior to that I was one of a team of curates in Scarborough who would undertake duties at parishes around the diocese. It so happened that in 'The Big Freeze' of 1947 I was called out to take a funeral here at Hunmanby. The local minister had been taken to hospital, and I was the only person available. I think your nocturnal visitor's name was, or is, Bill Pickering. He was a signalman here, like you."

You can imagine, by then I was getting excited by the vicar's revelations, but unfortunately, the bells started ringing, an' what with people coming to ask about what trains was running, an' what wasn't, I had to wait until next train had gone before the conversation could continue.

As the tail light of the train ghosted down the line towards Bridlington in a swirl of snow, I had barely tapped out 'train out of section' on the bells before I spun round and said "Well, he may be the man, but how can you be so sure. It was, let me see..."

With that, I paused, and counting to myself, I said "Sixteen years ago!"

"I'm certain he's your man, and I'll give you three reasons why" said the vicar authoritatively.

"Go on!" I winced, as the sudden sting of a hot spark from the fire nipped the back of my hand and made me jump.

"First, Bill Pickering was very pale. In fact, a number of people at the reception after the funeral told me his nickname was 'The Ghost!'

Secondly, it was one of the first funerals that I'd undertaken in my capacity as curate covering this parish. We buried him over there", pointing to the graveyard near the crossing gates.

"I'm still not convinced!" I replied firmly "Why does he

keep asking if owt's running?"

"Because the snow was so thick, I couldn't get here! Also, if I remember rightly, he died while trying to clear ice and snow off the signal wires. The train service had just been suspended and he was trying to do his bit to keep things going. Apparently, he was very conscientious" responded the vicar quickly.

"But why does he keep referring to meeting 'a person' " I said, rubbing the burn on my hand.

Eagerly rising to the bait, my visitor gushed forth "You yourself called me parson when I got off the train this morning. It's use is dying out now, but it was then a common greeting in these parts for ministers, and literally means 'THE PERSON'!"

It was now becoming clearer to me, but clutching at one final straw, for I just couldn't accept that I'd seen a ghost, I asked why he would want to return to his old workplace for three nights in succession.

After drinking the last of his now cold tea, the vicar continued "Your question brings me to my last point. Until I could get through on the early Scarborough train that day, which incidentally was the same one that I caught this morning, he'd lain for three days in Hunmanby Church."

"You mean...." I gasped.

"Yes!" interrupted the parson loudly "His funeral service was suspended for three days!"

# TERMINAL ILLNESS

"First aid to platform 8, I repeat, first aid urgently to platform 8". The disembodied voice came over the Tannoy, just after I'd stepped out of my office at the recently nationalised Kings Cross Station. This might require my services I thought to myself, as I strode purposefully across the station's large concourse.

Oh, I better introduce myself, I'm Jack Bentley, and I'm a member of the British Transport Police. I've been at 'The Cross' for the last ten years and I'm due to retire in two. Up until this message, it had just been another routine day at the famous ex-L.N.E.R., now B.R., terminus; two angry passengers, a few fare dodgers, a pickpocket and a consignment of wines had been 'misplaced'.

The Leeds express had just come in behind a Gresley Pacific when I arrived at the scene.

"T'owd chap's a gonner" came a down to earth Yorkshire voice from among a crowd that had gathered near the ticket barrier.

Asserting myself, I boomed out "Excuse me please, let me through!"

Seeing the uniform, the gathering edged aside, to reveal a man, who I assumed to be a doctor, giving first aid to someone lying on the ground.

"What's going on, then?" I said, as I hunched down to assist.

"Ah, hello officer, I don't think you'll be needed, it looks like a mild heart attack" said the smartly dressed gentleman holding the casualty's head.

"It's old Peter!" I exclaimed.

"You know him then?" replied the first-aider, introducing himself as Frank Simpson, a G.P. from the north.

"Everyone here at the Cross knows Peter".

"Well, he's old, but he'll pull through. He seems very tough for his age" said Doctor Simpson as the patient was lifted onto a stretcher and taken to a waiting ambulance.

As the casualty was carefully placed in the vehicle, Frank turned to me and said in a questioning voice "I've a few minutes to spare, so I'm curious to know about the old man".

When a story needs to be told, the British instinctively reach for a cup of tea, and so it was that five minutes later, we found ourselves in the warmth of the buffet.

Frank opened the conversation "Well, apart from being called Peter, who is the old fellow then?"

"In some ways it's easy to say, and in some ways, it's not" I said with a chuckle. "He's wandered around the station like a tramp ever since I've been here, and that's ten years, but the older staff say that he's hung around here as long as they can remember".

"Where does he live then?" replied Frank.

"I'm not sure, but he turns up here at almost any time of day or night. I think that he likes the company. We should really move him on, but he's never caused any harm or offence, and he can tell railway stories like a good 'un, mark my words!"

The young doctor, becoming more curious, asked "How does he live, or eat, or keep warm?"

"Ah, there's little problem there" I offered in reply "Railway folk can be very generous, and they often bring a little extra snap, you know, grub, for him. As to keeping warm, he often dozes in the porters' lobby if no one objects."

"With rationing still on, it's good to know that people can be generous enough to help out an old vagrant" Frank replied "Anyway, I must be off, but I hope someone looks up the old boy. A few days in hospital might do him a power of good, but it might be a bit lonely for an old timer who's used to railwaymens' company."

With that, the doctor bade me farewell and stepped out into the bustling concourse, waved goodbye, and was gone.

I returned to my office, made out my reports, and was just about to go home at the end of my shift when Reg Brierley, a shunter driver, dropped in. "I hear old Peter's badly, Jack. Is that right?"

"Aye, I've just checked up and they've taken him to Charing Cross Hospital for tests. He'll be in there a day or two they reckon".

Now Reg was a real kind hearted gent and replied "Someone'll have to make sure he's O.K. I finish in two hours, I'll drop in on 'im."

"Don't be daft, Reg, you live up in Finchley. It's miles out of your way, and anyway, your wife will be waiting for you" I replied. "I'm off now, and I've no one at home waiting for me, so I'll go."

"That's decent of you, Jack. I forgot that you live south of the river. But my offer still stands. I'm sure all the gang will put together a few tit-bits for Peter. Anyway, I'm off now. Keep us posted about the daft old beggar".
With that, Reg was off.

I put on my coat, said goodbye to a colleague, and strolled towards the underground.

"Don't forget to visit Old Peter!" cried Reg's voice from the footplate of his loco, just as it blew off steam.

"You can count on it!" I yelled back, above the roar of the safety valves.

Indeed, you could count on it, but not in the way that I had planned, for I never made it to the escalator. My head started spinning, and the last thing I remembered was whirling station lights and hitting the floor.


I awoke in a hospital bed. It was night, but the ward was still busy.

"Where am I?" I gasped.

"Charing Cross Hospital" replied the nurse at the next bed. "Don't you remember? You collapsed at Kings Cross station".

Blurred images started flooding back to me. "Ah, yes, I was heading for the underground when I was taken badly".

The nurse said cheerily "That's right, you're our second casualty from that station today".

I glanced to my right, and to my great surprise, there was old Peter!

"You're in safe hands here, Jack" came the old timer's reply.

116

"Well, fancy that! I was coming to see you, Peter, but not as a fellow patient. How are you doing?"

As the nurse checked his blood pressure, Peter piped up "Not bad, not bad. They've given me tests, and I'll probably be back to my old haunts in a day or two. What would you chaps at the Cross do without me to keep an eye on the place!"

"Yes, what indeed". I agreed, as I lay back on my pillow.

With that, the duty doctor arrived at my bedside "Hello, I'm Doctor Stephens. How are you feeling, Mr Bentley?"

"A little groggy. What happened doctor?"

"Nothing to worry about, just a mild heart attack, like your neighbour here. Not unusual at your age, it's nature's way of telling you to slow down a bit, or you won't live to Peter's age. You've got a strong constitution there!" chuckled the doctor, as he looked across at the veteran.

Raising myself on the bed, I enquired "When am I likely to be out then, doctor?"

"I see no problem in a day or two" he said, as he put his hands in his white jacket.

"That's good. I want to keep in good form, what with my retirement only two years away".

Walking off to visit another patient, he responded "I see no problem, if you look after yourself".

"Thank you, doctor, I'll sleep a lot easier tonight then" I said warmly.

However, the night was to be anything but easy.

Hospital time is long time, and after tossing and turning for what seemed hours, I eventually dropped off into slumber, but not for long.

"Hello, Jack, it's me, Peter".

Startled, I mumbled "Go back to bed, Peter, it's late".

"Later than you think, friend".

His voice had changed, and it chilled my soul.

"What do you mean? Go to bed. I want to get better and get out of here quickly".

Again, Peter's whispered words sent shivers down my spine "Aye, you'll get out of here quickly alright, but not the way you think!" My whole being froze in the bed as he continued "Didn't any of you fools wonder how I seem to have been around forever?"

"You heard the doctor, you're tough, full of life" I offered limply.

With eyes ablaze, he ominously spat out into my face "Yes, full of life - your life!"


"Hello, Peter, you're back!" called out Reg Brierley in surprise, as he bumped into the veteran on the way to the shunters' bothy at Kings Cross station. "If you carry on much longer we'll start to believe that you've sold your soul to the Devil!"

"Aye, I'm back, stronger than ever. You can't get rid of me that easily!" replied Peter with a mischievous smile.

Reg's face fell as he continued "Shame about Jack Bentley. You remember Jack, don't you? Doesn't make any sense, the hospital said that there was nothing much amiss with him. Never seen anything like it. A real surprise, he had nothing terminal".

His words almost lost in the bark of the exhaust of the Edinburgh express as it pulled out, Peter confided "Jack was always a favourite of mine, a real gentleman. He gave me a lot to live for".

Trying to cheer up the mood, Reg lifted his head and continued "Well, life has to go on!"

"Indeed it does" was Peter's reply.


"Platform 9 for the 19.33 Hull Trains service to Hull, calling at Grantham, Doncaster, Selby and Brough. Platform 9 for the 19.33 Hull Trains service to Hull" boomed out the public address system through the gloom of a January night at the recently privatised Kings Cross.

"You O.K., Dean?" said the old vagrant kindly.

"Hi, Peter, just been a bit off colour today. I'll be alright, my turn is just finishing. Anyway, on a cold night like this, you should be worrying about yourself, not me. You might have hung around the station for what seems like an eternity, but no one lives forever".

Rubbing his hands, and speaking with concern, Peter said "I'd never forgive myself if something happened to you on the way home, Dean. All the railwayman are like family to me here at the Cross, but you're my favourite. I'll make sure you get home in one piece".

"That's kind of you, Peter. I'll just get my things and we'll be off".

To the fanfare of diesel engines revving up, Dean slung his rucksack across his shoulders, and the odd couple, the old tramp and the young conductor, stepped out of the terminus and shuffled off into the night.

# THE CURSE OF THE BANKER

"This is totally unacceptable!" came an angry voice from the ticket barrier.

Defensively, the ticket inspector responded with the standard company line "I can assure you, sir, that the railway does everything within its power to ensure that services run to schedule."

The reply, like a bullet, cannoned back from a tall gentleman in a dark suit "But they don't!"

He was obviously not going to let the matter go, and with his black umbrella flailing like a demented raven, he ranted "Bring me the station master, and be quick about it!"

The other passengers, not wishing to be delayed any further on such a wet evening, filtered past the man, and trudged resignedly off home. They'd all gone by the time Mr Hodgson, the station master appeared on the scene.

With a conciliatory tone, he introduced himself and said "I can understand your irritation at arriving twenty minutes late home, but I am sure that there is a very genuine operational reason for your unfortunate delay."

The pompous man, rising to the challenge, inflated his chest and said dismissively "I doubt it".

"We shall see" was the guarded response from the seasoned railwayman, who had only been in charge of the town terminus for a month.

"Fetch me the driver and fireman of the 5.12 pm service" he said to a passing porter, who promptly walked towards the railwayman's mess room.

Pointing at a black door between the newsagent's stall and the buffet, Mr Hodgson continued "Come with me sir, to my office, where I am sure that we can have the matter resolved to your satisfaction".

Once seated in his office, Mr Hodgson tried to take control by noting down all the relevant facts of the complaint on an official form.

"Name please?"

"Don't you know who I am?" came the unhelpful reply.

"Sir, for us to process your complaint, we really need to proceed in the approved manner".

The belligerent man blustered "Oh, all right, my name is Mr Stephenson, Nigel Stephenson".

After a short pause, there was a glimmer of recognition in Mr Hodgson's eyes. Tentatively, he said "Mr Stephenson of the local bank?"

This seemed to appease the combatant somewhat, and for the first time he relaxed a little. "Yes, I am Mr Stephenson, the manager of the branch on Market Street" and pointing his brolly at the besieged station master, he continued "And I am not used to being delayed in my daily routine".

Mr Hodgson noted down the relevant details of the complaint as the irate banker continued his tirade against British Railways, and this branch line in particular.

A knock on the door provided a welcome relief for the station master, who was beginning to tire. Politely, he summoned those waiting outside "Please come in".

Two railwaymen in blue overalls stepped into the room and removed their caps.

The taller and older of the two, Driver Jack Greaves, blurted out "What's the problem Guvn'r?"

"This gentleman is very annoyed at the delayed arrival of your train tonight. I know that you'll be filling out the relevant records for the authorities, but I would like to hear your explanation now, so that I can process this complaint form."

The younger chap, Fireman Dave Birkin, leapt in with their defence "It's that blasted final climb into here. The loco lost its feet three times on the ascent, an' finally came to a standstill near the distant signal. We gave the sanding gear some real stick an' got her started agin, but when it's as wet as it is today, we have a real job on just keeping goin".

"Aye, that's right" added Jack Greaves "We 'ad six on t'night, and the book on'y stipulates five up the bank!"

Hoping to appease Mr Stephenson, Mr Hodgson seized the moment.

"It's obviously a combination of the weather and overloading. I shall contact the Operating Department and see if we can ensure that there is not a repetition of tonight's unfortunate events".

Any hopes of reconciliation were immediately dashed by the banker's response.

"The railway can't control the trains, let alone the weather. As for fewer coaches, it's already bad as it is. I had to stand all the way tonight. I'm not paying good money for an even poorer service. You had better come up with something better than that!"

Mr Hodgson's face fell, and the train crew, realising the difficulty he was under, tried to offer a ray of hope in the situation.

"How about a banker!" said Jack.

"Aye, that would help" added Dave.

The puzzled financier looked up, muttering "I beg your pardon!"

Stepping in here, Hodgson explained "He means a banking engine. It's a railway term for a locomotive positioned at the rear of the train to assist up a steep incline. It's not unusual, but I doubt that the authorities would sanction the use on our branch, it would be too costly".

"Damn the cost!" exploded Mr Stephenson, rising to his feet.

This was too much for Jack Greaves, who'd met some awkward customers in his time, and was getting rankled by the man's arrogance. "Who the Hell do you think you are, the King of Prussia? You can't come in here telling us how to do our jobs! We're on'y trying to help".

"Please gentlemen, calm down!" said the exasperated station master, but to no avail.

The banker strode to the door before turning, and then said ominously "You haven't heard the last of me. I have connections you know. We'll see about a banking locomotive indeed!"

Then, pointing his black brolly like a weapon at Jack Greaves, he hissed darkly "And as for you, don't think I'll forget you. I'll not tolerate your kind of insolence".

With a slam of the door, he departed, and all three men were left to ponder what it all meant.

The station master was conciliatory "Sorry about that. He certainly got himself into a state. However, I don't think it'll come to much".

"Don't be too sure" replied Jack sullenly "He's been at the bank here for three years an' he has a reputation for being a hard taskmaster. What's more, he does have connections, for it's his bank that supplies our weekly wages. I think he plays golf with the Divisional Manager".

Wishing the matter to go no further, Dave Birkin added "Is that all sir? We better be off now, 'cos our hours are up, aren't they Jack?"

The driver nodded agreement.

Mr Hodgson dismissed the two men, and leaning around his office door called after them "Don't forget to fill out your running reports!"

Life returned to normal in the town. Or not quite normal, for true to his word, Mr Stephenson had not let the matter drop. In the footnotes for the winter operating timetable, commencing September 12$^{th}$, were the words - 'Banker to be supplied at foot of incline for 5.12 pm train'.

So he'd got his way. Were there no limits to the influence this man had? Well, yes, there were, for as autumn turned to winter, dark rumours surfaced that all was not well at the bank.

However, few of the townsfolk were prepared for the headline in the December 19$^{th}$ newspaper -

'Irregularities at local bank. Manager suspended'.

A stark message indeed. How were the mighty fallen! The police were called in and it was rumoured that there was a considerable discrepancy in the accounts. Mr Stephenson was questioned and then released on bail, pending preliminary hearings.

Mr Hodgson had followed the proceedings with considerable interest, for the man was certainly one of the more cussed people that he had met. However, interest turned to utter disbelief when he answered the telephone late on December 21$^{st}$.

"Hodgson here, how can I help?"

It's amazing how thirty seconds can change a man's life, and the conversation that followed did that all right.

"You what! Where?" Then after a pause "How?"

The railwayman slumped back in his chair, and the telephone receiver fell from his hands as he stared blankly through the window at the signal lights punctuating the darkness at the end of the platform.

All was revealed in the following day's local rag - 'Banker found dead. Suicide suspected'.

It appears that the decapitated body of Mr Stephenson had been found next to the track at the foot of the incline. The crew of the banking locomotive had reported a bump when they steamed back down the bank after pushing the 5.12 pm into the terminus. They stopped to investigate and found the gruesome wreck of this once formidable man. Questions were asked. What had he been doing there, and why at such a strange hour? Surely the inquest would reveal all.

His widow could add little. Yes, he had been very distressed at the investigation, but seemed reasonably cheerful in the circumstances, for he was a very determined man. Why he had gone to such a lonely spot, in the dark, she could only guess at. So the verdict was reached 'Accidental death, probably suicide while balance of mind was disturbed'. Any hope of recovering the missing money, confirmed by then at no less than £20,000, died with the culprit.

Winter turned to spring, life returned to normal and the grizzly fate of the unfortunate financier dropped from the conversation of ordinary folks as the long summer months arrived. However, there is a season for everything, and for everything a season, and so a gruesome anniversary rapidly approached once more.

On December 21st, Jack Greaves and Dave Birkin were rostered for the 5.12 pm. As had become regular practice, they stopped at the foot of the incline and sounded out the requisite number of 'crows', that is, long whistles, for the banker to buffer up. It was a dreadful night, for a real pea-souper fog had descended on the hills and they could hardly see signal lights, let alone dirty steam locos. There was the customary jolt as the banking engine connected with the rear of the commuter train.

"A bit brutal that" said Jack over the noise of the footplate.

"Oh, he's just keen to give us a shove up an' get off home" was Dave's cheery reply.

Jack blew the whistle, and within a couple of seconds the expected reply screeched through the mist behind them.

"We're away!" Jack said, as he opened the regulator. The train seemed to buck as the combined power of the two locomotives got to grips with the train.

All was not right though.

"He's pushing damn hard!" Dave yelled as they sped up the gradient.

"A little too hard for my liking" came Jack's anxious reply.

Before long the crocodile of ageing coaches was ascending the bank at a terrifying pace.

"What's his game!" screamed Jack, as he notched the regulator back, trying to slow the ascent.

Dave peered futilely back "I don't know, but at this rate we'll struggle to stop. We need a good sighting of the distant signal!"

Jack's eyes streamed as he tried to recognise familiar landmarks "That'll be tricky in this fog. I hope there's fogmen out with detonators!"

Well, there were no fogmen using exploding detonators at key locations to assist train crews that evening. The fog had descended too suddenly to call men out in time. The crew of the banking engine disregarded all attempts by Dave and Jack to communicate with them or slow down. So the stage was set for disaster. They over ran the distant signal and tore into the terminus at thirty miles an hour, despite all endeavours by the two men with the brake, and even the reversing gear.

The 5.12 pm hit the buffers and ploughed into the platform beyond. Jack Greave's head hit the locomotive cabside as he was thrown into the debris. Luckily, Dave Birkin had braced himself against the impact, and only suffered a broken wrist. The train behind piled up in an ugly mess.

Mr Hodgson ran out of his office "What the hell!"

Upon seeing the devastation, he ran to Fireman Birkin, who nursing his wrist, was stumbling through the wreckage.

"Help Jack!" cried Dave, as the station master ran towards the prone body of his mate.

Jack was in a bad way "What's the banker's game?" he kept repeating over and over.

The professionalism in Hodgson came to the fore, as he strode purposefully to his office and contacted the emergency services. He then called up on the 'phone all local staff who could help in a situation like this, while attempting to answer the many questions thrown at him by staff, police and ambulance crew as they burst through his door.

For an hour it was pure bedlam, and then it settled down to just chaos. Picking up the telephone for the umpteenth time, Hodgson heard with great sadness that Jack Greaves hadn't made it. Fortunately, it appeared that there were no fatalities among the passengers of the ill-fated train. Dave was still in his office, having refused to go the hospital so that he could help. "There's more needy people than me on the train" was his stoic reply.

The station master sat next to Dave and speaking very softly he said "I'm afraid that Jack didn't make it, too many internal injuries. Kept ranting about the banker". There was a pause.

"What's he going on about the banker for?"

Dave looked up, puzzled "The one pushing us up the incline like the Devil".

It was Mr Hodgson's turn to be perplexed.

"But there was no loco available tonight. Control rang at 4.30 pm. They had a crew sick, with no relief men available in time. What banker are you on about?"

Dave rose stiffly from the comfort of the chair, and the two men stepped out of the warmth of the office, through the wreckage, and past the rescue crews towards the place where the offending engine should be located.

Even in the gloom and mist, it was obvious there was no locomotive. There was the rear of the damaged train, with the tail-light still giving out its warning red glow.

"But, what pushed......" Here Dave's voice trailed away to a whisper and the fireman crumpled to his knees.

Hodgson knelt down, and touching his shoulder, he said sympathetically "It's been a long day for you. Get some rest. I'm sure we'll soon find an explanation".

With that, an ambulance man walked up and said to Dave "You really should come with us, sir. There just might be more damage than your wrist".

Dave was past caring and he just collapsed onto the stretcher offered to him. Two men were soon striding down the platform, the fireman's damaged arm hanging limply from one side.

There was a preliminary hearing in the town hall the following week, to gather evidence and interview witnesses. Dave Birkin was well enough to add his pennyworth, but despite all his protestations, it was clearly established that no banking locomotive had been available on that fateful night. What did send more than a ripple through the officials gathered there, was the testimony of Jeff Coates, the track walker for the stretch of line that included the foot of the incline.

On the morning of December 22$^{nd}$, he'd walked past the spot where the banker usually stabled before assisting the train in question. Something on the ballast at the side of the track, in what railwaymen call 'the cess' had caught his eye. It was a black umbrella. He swore under oath that it hadn't been there the day before. When he had picked up the brolly, he noticed a package protruding from a small culvert down the bank. You can almost hear the gasps of amazement in the town hall when the officials revealed that it contained notes to the value of £20,000!

Had the banker had the last word?

# BEYOND THE END OF THE LINE

There once existed a little railway that literally was 'beyond the end of the line'. It was the Spurn Military Railway, built in the First World War to help defend Britain from potential threats from across the North Sea. Running from Kilnsea to Spurn Point on the Yorkshire coast, its nearest connection to the national system was over ten miles away at Patrington, just short of the branch terminus at Withernsea. Some still have memories of this fascinating line at such a remote location.

Bill Hartley's Christmas Eve party was in full swing, when, having had a little too much to drink, his mates egged him on to tell a story from his army days in World War Two.

"Come on Bill, tell us about the time you were stationed at Spurn Point", said Jim, who by midnight was well-oiled.

"O.K., an' it's the right time of year for this particular tale!" came Bill's reply, but hesitating for a moment, he replied seriously "What I'm gonna tell you is the gospel truth, but I still doubt you'll believe me."

Everyone was intrigued now, and when all in the room had calmed down and looked suitably serious, Bill took a bite out of his mince pie, and started his story.

"December 1940 found me based at the Green Battery, which were the fortifications at the tip of Spurn Point. Me an' my mate, Archie Ramsbottom, we were responsible for the motive power on the military line that ran to the Godwin Battery at Kilnsea. That is, we worked on the locos. Now, as luck would have it, we were ordered by the sergeant on Christmas Eve to take a loco out".

"What's up?" I said to the sergeant, as me and Archie trudged down to the engine shed through driving rain. "The sea's trying to break through near Kilnsea Warren. Get some sandbags and gear from stores and proceed up there" yelled the sergeant through the wind. "And make it smartish!"

With that he marched off quickly to the party that was going full swing in the mess hut, leaving us to prepare the engine.

Taking a sup of his ale, Bill continued "We had a steam engine at that time, borrowed from the L.N.E.R. at Hull Dairycoates Depot. It was a little tank loco, number 559, which we nick-named 'Black Sapper'. I remember it well, because I had to fill in all the repair logs at the time. It took time to get up steam, and so it was well after midnight before the little engine trundled out of the shed and onto what passed as the main line on that windswept spit of land. Now, we were more used to working with internal combustion engines than steam, and so as we set off into the northerly storm, 'Black Sapper' steamed very badly for us. In fact, we were getting more sparks out of chimney than we were getting steam into cylinders!"

'Not steaming well!' yelled Archie to me across the cab as he stoked her up.

"No, we're lighting up the sky wi' flame. Hope Gerry's not out tonight, or we'll be a sitting target for 'im!" I replied.

"We'd gone a mile or a bit more, when we went into a proper sea rauk, a right mist. It seemed as though the storm had died down a bit, and it all went quietish, in fact, a bit freaky. The track beneath our wheels seemed not right, so we got down off the loco to take a look. Well, the sea was trying to break through alright, but it wasn't that which caught our attention so much as what was in the sea. At first we thought it must be Gerry making an invasion attempt, but that would have been almost welcome to what we really saw".

"What was it?" came an impatient shout from Bill's nephew, Adrian, who up until then had been busy watching T.V. and feeding his face.

"Coffins!" Bill spluttered, as he took a quick bite out his pie.

Adrian didn't hesitate with his reply "You're kidding!"

"No, I'm not! I told you, you wouldn't believe me" said Bill, somewhat miffed at his nephew's rebuke. Now Adrian was not his favourite relative, seeing he'd deserted the side and moved down south.

"You're all daft in the head up here in Yorkshire!" was Adrian's cocky reply, as he turned round to watch yet another repeat on the box.

Rattled, Bill finished off his mince pie, and tried to pick up the thread of the story again.

"Come on!" uttered Jim "You can eat later, we're all dead

keen to hear what you've got to say now!"

Bill composed himself and continued "Well, the line ahead 'ad disappeared, 'an where it should have been, was a scene that beggared belief."

'What the 'ell!' my mate Archie gasped, as we stared at folk dressed in tatters trying to drag coffins from the waves, with only flickering lanterns for light. We could hardly believe our eyes.

Rushing towards us was a man, who judging from his clothes was a priest. Bursting with fury, and with his wild eyes filled with fear, he screamed at me and Archie. 'Get hence, ye foul demons of the night! We have seen the Devil's chariot, in smoke and flames bring you here. Our good Lord may be calling us all to judgement on this day, but His mercy will surely protect us from thee!' His voice rising in pitch, he screamed 'Yea, though it be the end of the world, we will not bow to thee! Be gone!' With that, the priest in a frenzy of rage and a further torrent of oaths hurled his crucifix at us.

Here Bill paused, as all in the room were silent. That is, apart from Adrian, who was chuckling to himself, transfixed by the idiotic ramblings coming from the T.V.. Mopping his brow with his party hat, Bill piped up once more.

"We didn't need 'im telling us t' go. Yon priest might 'ave thought it was the end of the world, but so did we! We were off like greyhounds t' loco! Archie fell over the sleepers, but I grabbed 'im, an' we was off as fast as that little loco could go. When we got back to the depot we said nowt t' anyone, 'cos as you can imagine, they'd all

think we'd gone barmy".
Adrian's attack was swift "And they'd be right!"

"Just ignore 'im" said Jim, unruffled. "He's only young an' daft. Get on wi' story, it's getting more and more interesting!"
Supping some more ale, and then dipping into the crisps on the table, Bill chirped up "Thanks, Jim. Well next morning, Christmas Day, we took number 559 down the line again. We got near Kilnsea Warren, jumped off the loco and put down some of the sandbags that we should have dumped the night before. All seemed normal until we stumbled back to the engine. There on some sea buckthorn was a crucifix! We grabbed it, and off we trundled back to Spurn".
'What do you think we should do now?' asked Archie as we got down off the loco's footplate.
"I thought to mi'self for a moment", then I replied "I reckon I know the man who can help, we'll have to wait for an hour or two".

After the regular Christmas service, we collared the Army Chaplain and told him our story, as we knew he was an educated man, an' being discreet, we were confident that it would go no further.
To our surprise, he didn't mock us, but thought for a while and said, 'Come with me to my room. I think it is best that we talk there. As we walked down the corridor, he turned and commented 'By the way, chaps, that was some storm last night. I haven't seen the barometer so low for many a year!'

Once there, he made a pot of tea, and while we waited for it to brew, he told us that along with astronomy, the history of the East Riding of Yorkshire was one of his hobbies. He then took an old book down from the shelves, and flicking through the dusty pages, I remember he muttered to us 'Did you know that Mars is in conjunction with the first quarter of the Moon today?"

We both looked at each other, puzzled, before I replied "No, I didn't, does that mean summat, then?"

He chuckled and added 'No, I don't think so, but you never know.' He paused, then continued 'It sounds to me that what you probably witnessed was a scene from Ravenser Odd in the 14th century'.

'Ravens what?' was Archie's reply, an' to tell the truth it was mine as well.

The Chaplain continued 'Ravenser Odd was a town that threatened to put both Hull and Grimsby out of business. It was a flourishing port about that time, with a weekly market, a yearly fair, and representation at Parliament. The land on which it stood seemed to be cast up by the sea about 1230, and the town prospered for a hundred years, It was the end of the line for Ravenser Odd when it got swept away by the sea, some time around 1360.'

The Chaplain paused, and chuckling to himself, said 'It was like a 'modern day' Atlantis, relatively speaking that is, in history terms'.

'No wonder we've never heard of it!' said Archie an' me together. 'But what about all the coffins in the sea?'

The Chaplain was ready for us.

'In 1355 the sea overran Ravenser, flooded the graveyard

and 'resurrected the dead' by lifting the coffins from their 'final' resting places. The deceaseds' resurrection was short lived however, as they were soon reburied at places such as Kilnsea and Easington. The priest could have been helping the townsfolk reclaim their loved ones when you two hove into sight. He probably did think that it was the end of the world, and in his mind, your appearance riding a chariot of fire naturally confirmed this opinion.'

Here Archie butted in. With a laugh, he blurted out 'When we were sent to Spurn Point and stationed at Green Battery, we knew it were the end of Yorkshire, but we didn't expect to get the end o' the world as well!' This amused everyone, and as the Chaplain poured the by now well stewed tea, he continued 'After the town was washed away, the chronicles of the time suggest that Ravenser was destroyed because of its evil ways.' Supping on my mug of char, I butted in "You mean like piracy, an' that sort of thing?" 'It was apparently home to some less than savoury folks, and so I wouldn't be surprised if piracy was among their particular talents' replied the Chaplain with a smile. After that, the conversation between the three of us rambled off into more traditional army territory, "Y'know, stuff like rations, leave and suchlike."

At this point, Bill, confident that his tale had had the required impact, opened another ale, and proclaimed confidently to his gathered friends, who by now were

all deep in thought "So that explained it".
This statement caused howls of laughter in the room,
even from nephew Adrian.

But did it? Occasionally, lengths of old track are exposed
for a short while by the sea, only to be lost again after a
few days. So, for a fleeting moment, one can glimpse a
little fragment of the Spurn Military Railway. However,
what temporal aberration caused a seven hundred year
old event to be re-enacted? As the noise of the party
swelled around him, Bill looked into his beer and
pondered. He then sat down and flicked desultorily
through Adrian's posh newspaper. Whether by fate, or
by chance, the pages fell open at the astronomical notes
for the month. There, large as life, was the entry 'Mars
in conjunction with the Moon on the 25th'. A shudder
ran through Bill's body, and glancing at the barometer,
which was falling rapidly, he looked towards the
window, and out into the icy December night.

Lightning Source UK Ltd.
Milton Keynes UK
UKOW04f1426081113

220644UK00001B/13/P